What the critics are saying…

"What can I say but *Mr. Gabriel* has amazed me again with his wonderful tale of grand adventure with a great paranormal twist. With love scenes as hot as the desert the story is set in and action that just doesn't seem to stop the *Prisoner of Shera-Sa* is an impressive story of a love that conquers all…The only thing I have left to say is move over Rick O'Connell and Indiana Jones because a new mummy hunter has hit the scene and he is one hot number." ~ *Raven Jackman Romance Junkies Reviewer*

"Minarra and Mac's relationship is volatile and steamy. The reader will be left looking for a fan after reading some of their sex scenes. *Reese Gabriel* knows how to mix suspense and sex together to make a great page turner of a book. The author delves into the hidden passions of the characters and splashes them on the pages of the book." ~ *Candy, eCataRomance reviews*

The Prisoner of Shera-Sa is an exciting and hot adventure story. Between trekking across the desert, fighting gun-toting rebels, evil ghosts, and incredibly hot sex; there is hardly a lull in the excitement. It is like a sinfully erotic Indiana Jones. The sexual tension between Mac and Minarra is shiver inducing and hotter than the desert Shera-Sa is buried in. ~ *D.J.,Reviewer for Karen Find Out About New Books, Reviewer for Coffee Time Romance*

"Mr. Gabriel blends action and romance with the *Prisoner of Shera-Sa*. Mac and Minarra belong together, but old secrets and hurt has kept them apart....The story flows at a good pace and the love scenes are sizzling with D/s elements in keeping with the storyline." ~ *Luisa, Cupid's Library Reviews*

Reese Gabriel

Prisoner of Shera-Sa

Ellora's Cave
Romantica Publishing

An Ellora's Cave Romantica Publication

www.ellorascave.com

Prisoner of Shera-Sa

ISBN #1419953176
ALL RIGHTS RESERVED.
Prisoner of Shera-Sa Copyright© 2005 Reese Gabriel
Edited by: Pamela Campbell
Cover art by: Syneca

Electronic book Publication: June, 2005
Trade paperback Publication: December, 2005

Excerpt from *Dance of Submission*
Copyright © Reese Gabriel, 2004
Excerpt from *Come and Get Me* Copyright © Reese Gabriel, 2005

With the exception of quotes used in reviews, this book may not be reproduced or used in whole or in part by any means existing without written permission from the publisher, Ellora's Cave Publishing, Inc.® 1056 Home Avenue, Akron OH 44310-3502.

This book is a work of fiction and any resemblance to persons, living or dead, or places, events or locales is purely coincidental. The characters are productions of the authors' imagination and used fictitiously.

Warning:

The following material contains graphic sexual content meant for mature readers. *Prisoner of Shera-Sa* has been rated *E--rotic* by a minimum of three independent reviewers.

Ellora's Cave Publishing offers three levels of Romantica™ reading entertainment: S (S-ensuous), E (E-rotic), and X (X-treme).

S-*ensuous* love scenes are explicit and leave nothing to the imagination.

E-*rotic* love scenes are explicit, leave nothing to the imagination, and are high in volume per the overall word count. In addition, some E-rated titles might contain fantasy material that some readers find objectionable, such as bondage, submission, same sex encounters, forced seductions, etc. E-rated titles are the most graphic titles we carry; it is common, for instance, for an author to use words such as "fucking", "cock", "pussy", etc., within their work of literature.

X-*treme* titles differ from E-rated titles only in plot premise and storyline execution. Unlike E-rated titles, stories designated with the letter X tend to contain controversial subject matter not for the faint of heart.

Also by Reese Gabriel:

Come and Get Me
Dance of Submission
Kimberlee's Keeper
Roping His Filly
Temporary Slave

Prisoner of Shera-Sa

Chapter One

Doctor Minarra Hunt was beyond fuming by the time she reached the Archeology Department office. "Don't bother telling him I'm here," she stormed past the chairman's frizzy-haired secretary Freida. "He'll only try and run out the back door."

"Minarra," Dr. Malcolm Rey braced himself as she breached the inner sanctum, an odd assortment of relics and artifacts bound by walls of books, stacked seven feet high with priceless volumes bound in red, blue and green leather. "Just give me a chance to explain…"

The raven-haired expert on lost civilizations glared through ice blue eyes. "Explain?" She tossed the memo onto the polished mahogany desk, covered at the moment with photocopied hieroglyphic scrolls representing the myriad self-proclaimed accomplishments of Pharaoh Tutensahet IV. "What's to explain? I think treason speaks for itself quite nicely."

Professor Rey held out a pair of small, elflike hands, untrained for any sort of physical labor. His curly red hair and beard were turning gray now, but his eyes still held the passion of a young man. "Minarra, be reasonable…"

"I'm tired of being reasonable, Malcolm. Time and again, I have been overlooked because of my sex and my lineage and I won't let it happen anymore. Especially not with this. You know what heading up this expedition means to me — my father gave his life looking for Shera-Sa…"

Malcolm's brow pinched. He'd been a professor at the university for twenty-five years, the last ten as chair of the department. "Of course, I know what it means, Minarra. I was one of your father's oldest friends and supporters. And I am also your godfather, may I point out. One of the last things he ever said to me was to watch out for your safety. You are just like your mother, he said. Brave, beautiful and impulsive... This trip is fraught with danger. There is no telling what will be encountered out there in the desert, not to mention the towns. Alcazara is a dangerous place, Minarra. People die out there. I'm not saying you can't go, I just want to be sure we have someone...skilled to handle difficulties."

"And by skilled," she scorned, "you mean a man."

"It's not about gender." The five-foot-one-inch Malcolm pushed his spectacles defensively up the bridge of his button nose. He'd had this same pair for as long as she could remember. He'd also been wearing various versions of that same rumpled tweed jacket. "It is purely a matter of qualifications."

"In that case," she sought to trump his logic. "You'll have to give the job to me. I know more about Shera-Sa than anyone on the planet. Plus I am fluent in all relevant ancient and modern languages. Who can possibly match that?"

"No one," concurred a male voice from the doorway. "Then again, how are you at handling bandit caravans, rebel tribes and back alley cutthroats?"

Minarra's heart stopped in her chest. She was hearing things... She had to be. There was no way it could be...*him.*

"Hello, Minarra," rasped Seth "Mac" Macallister as she steeled her courage to turn and face him. "You're looking good."

And you're looking like a snake in the grass. You no-good, heartbreaking, sorry excuse for a human being...

Minarra cursed the unfairness of it all. The least this man could have done over the last half-decade was to turn into a hideous toad. Instead, he had only grown more sculpted, handsome, more classically gorgeous, his brush cut, sandy hair a perfect compliment to his light, desert kissed skin. His eyes were blue like hers, but paler. She had often seen the stars reflected in those eyes. He'd been alive as no other man she'd seen, before or since.

His body hadn't suffered any, either. He was lean, his sleek muscles kept in excellent shape beneath his old familiar khakis. How well she knew the feel of those smooth pectorals, so warm to the touch, as she would search out his heartbeat with the palms of her hands. And his biceps that curled into steel and the hands, weathered, with the fingers of a man, capable of hard work and hard love. He'd taken her soul with those hands just as he'd taken her virginity with that sly cock, nine inches plus of hard, throbbing bliss between her undergraduate thighs. She'd bled for him. She'd come for him. She'd wept for him.

"Malcolm, I won't work with this man," she declared, summoning every ounce of her resistive strength. "Furthermore, if he is allowed anywhere near this project, I will resign and seek funding elsewhere for the expedition."

The dean's expression showed pain and bafflement. How could Minarra even begin to explain her personal sentiments to him when Malcolm knew nothing of their secret affair much less its horrid end? Being an academic by nature, Malcolm was ill-equipped and loath to deal with the vagaries of human emotion as it was. Minarra understood the feeling well. Like the rest of their kind, he preferred long-dead civilizations, where intrigues and agonies and treasons could be studied *ex post facto* in the quiet of one's laboratory, or better still one's study over gentle lamplight.

"But why on earth would you do that, Minarra?" he asked, obviously hoping to avoid any real conflict. "Dr. Macallister is just the sort of person we need. He's spent time in Alcazara. He's lived with the people there and he knows the political situation. He's been in the middle of shooting wars and sandstorms and more things than I can name. And I certainly don't need to remind you that he spent time under your father's tutelage—the same as you?"

Malcolm might as well have taken a knife and plunged it into her breast. As if she needed to be reminded that this damnably handsome, strong and ferociously clever man had worked with her father, accompanying them on his last expedition to North Africa six years ago, and that she—a starry eyed undergraduate—had fallen head over heels?

Minarra folded her arms over her breasts. The way he used to touch them, as if they had been made for him. The way they had responded, the tiny rosebud nipples peaking almost instantly, her back arching, her mouth, forming a small, involuntary O. The way he made her ache. The smile of supreme satisfaction on his face as he won from her that small moan he would always wait for, before proceeding lower on her body. It was all so fresh, even now...

"I am quite familiar with *Doctor* Macallister's work. He's the "real-life Indiana Jones," complete with his own TV cult following," she fought the flush on her cheeks as the memories flooded. "Just what we need to legitimize our already shaky reputation in the scientific community. I'm sure he'll be able to make Shera-Sa as much of a popular laughingstock as Bigfoot or the Loch Ness Monster."

"Minarra," said Malcolm, "that's not a fair thing to say. Simply because Dr. Macallister has made archeology accessible to the public is no reason to denigrate his scientific commitment or abilities."

Minarra winced. He was right, of course. She was bordering on spitefulness—acting like one of those petty, tenure-glomming academics she despised so much. It was true she had objections to his selection for the job over her, but obviously there were personal issues involved.

Which surprised her, because she had thought herself to be over this man a long time ago.

"It's all right," said Mac. "I'm pretty thick-skinned by now."

"No, it's not all right," she snapped, irritated beyond measure at his attempt to look like the bigger person. "I was out of line. I owe you an apology."

He inclined his head. "Accepted."

"So do we have something here to build on?" Malcolm asked, the pleading in his voice only marginally disguised. "We've reached some…resolution?"

"I have no problems," said Mac, hands on his lean waist. "I am here to do a job."

Minarra narrowed her gaze. *How admirable of him*, she thought bitterly, *considering he was getting it all his way. As usual.*

"I'm here for the same job," she informed him. "And I can assure you, I will do it to the best of my ability."

"Well, there we have it," Malcolm ignored the emotional subtext entirely. "I trust you two can draw up the details of the expedition?"

"Absolutely," Mac nodded his absolutely photogenic head. "We can be ready in ten days."

"That's too long." Minarra shook out her mane of black hair as both men turned their eyes to her. "We need to leave in a week or less. You said yourself, Malcolm, that the situation is volatile. Suppose the terrain is wiped fresh by a sandstorm, or our contacts there meet some untimely end at the hands of bandits?"

Malcolm cleared his throat. "Mac, can you hire the men you need by then? Get the supplies?"

Mac pursed his lips very slightly. To an untrained observer it meant nothing, but for Minarra it was a clear sign the man was struggling with whether or not to voice his real opinion.

Go on, she dared him silently. *Try and defy me.*

The man's answer was as disarming as it was simple. "Yes," he said, his voice steady and true. "I can."

Her breathing quickened just a little. Never had she encountered a man whose sexuality emanated so completely from his whole being. Just watching that determination on his face, the way his brow knitted, she could imagine him running it all through his mind right now, determining the feasibility. Back in her father's camp in North Africa, Mac Macallister had been, among other things, in charge of the native laborers. They would have died for him, to a man, because he never once asked them to do something unless he'd already proved to them, and himself, that he could do twice as much.

Could he do the impossible and prepare an expedition of this size in that short a time? If he said so…then he could.

If only his word had any value when it came to the opposite sex.

"I want in on every step," she told him. "I want full veto power over everything. And when it comes to the archeological work itself, I call the shots. No ifs, ands or buts."

"Minarra…" Malcolm sought to rein her in. "I've already told you. Mac has to take command. The university board is firm on this. And the grant foundation, too."

"It's not a problem," Mac forestalled her intended vitriolic. "We'll be able to work together. You have my guarantee."

Malcolm took his extended hand, shaking on it. "I'm relieved, Mac. You have no idea."

"Glad to hear it, Malcolm. I know how important this is to you and to the university. Not to mention to Roger's memory. I'm honored, truly."

"No, Mac, we're the ones who are honored," said Malcolm. "I know that Roger saw you as a son in many ways."

Minarra clenched her fists. Granted, Malcolm didn't know about her and Mac's affair, but still, this sudden exercise of male bonding was seriously messing with her composure. Not to mention the fifty percent Greek temper she'd inherited from her mother.

How was it that men always managed to unite forces leaving any woman in the cold, while women had the devil of a time ever joining forces against men?

"Well, I guess that seals the deal. I'll leave you boys to smoke some cigars or putt some golf balls. If you need me, I'll be in my office finishing the translation of the map we're going to need to actually find Shera-Sa."

She was already at the door when she turned back for a parting shot. "By the way, in case you've both forgotten, the Roger Hunt whose name you are throwing around as if I wasn't even here, also happened to be my father."

"But, Minarra, wait..." Malcolm's appeal was in vain. Minarra was already too deep into that pit of emotions from which no amount of reason could extricate her. Sofia, her mother, had lived in that place, and ultimately died there.

And there'd been nothing her father could do to stop it. If only he could have forgiven himself, not driven himself so hard the last decade of his life. To his dying breath, he'd blamed his own career, his lifelong obsession with the lost city of Shera-Sa, the desert kingdom older than the Egyptians and thought to be the seeding agent of Mesopotamian civilization.

But Minarra had learned that there were things in the human psyche too deep to understand, let alone control. Her mother's suicide was no one's fault. It was a choice, made for unknown reasons. Maybe it could have been prevented if they'd had some of the medicines and treatments currently available.

Her own answer to the mystery had been to pick up her father's work, taking it not to the brink of madness, but to its rigorous, scientific conclusion. If the so-called "missing link" did not exist to explain the near simultaneous arising of civilization in five areas of the world, then she would find out conclusively. Either way, she would lay the ghost to rest.

She, not Malcolm, and especially not Mac.

She might have to accept his place on the team, but she did not have to roll over and play dead. She would be hard-nosed with him, every bit as intimidating as her father.

To do this she would have to stay objective, firm and on her guard. And above all, without exception, she must not allow herself to be at all attracted to Mac again.

No matter how good looking he was now, no matter how well he'd aged, and no matter how damned lonely she was and physically needy. Just the thought of him laying a hand on her the way he used to, those fingers of his igniting her, creating soul-deep itches that only he could scratch…

The way he had stood with her outside her tent under the silver-flecked black onyx sky, surrounded by deathly silent sand, holding her body against the surprising desert chill that first night. Drawing her in, absorbing the light from her wide, curious eyes.

And those words he'd whispered into her ear, his lips barely grazing her hot blood-flushed earlobe. "Let me be the one."

The first.

As it had turned out, he'd been the only one, too, though she would never, ever give him the satisfaction of knowing how thoroughly he had spoiled her for other men. After all this time, the idea of ever drawing another man inside her, of opening herself for a new shaft, filled her with such a sense of indescribable sadness.

The therapist she'd seen had lots of fancy names for it. Displacement syndrome, unresolved emotional issues. But that woman had never been made love to by the likes of Mac Macallister. She'd like to see her use her fancy phrases after a night in his bed, after being taught, part-by-part, what her body was all about and how it could be made to respond.

Mac used to joke with her about making his mark. Putting a brand on her that would seal her as his woman. Forever. He'd gone so far as to tell her the practice among some of the Bedouin tribesmen of burning identifying marks into the flesh of their females.

It was nothing that would ever happen in real life, but he'd only ever had to touch her lightly on her thigh, or her ass, to remind her of the symbolism, the power of the fantasy. One of his favorite things to do had been to come up behind her while she was trying to work.

"Morning, baby," he would kiss her earlobe, pressing his thumb against her bare thigh, just below the hem of her shorts.

She'd melt on the spot, a wreck for hours afterward. He got a kick out of it, making her follow him around, begging for stolen midday sex away from the eyes and ears of the others, particularly her father.

Minarra had managed some teasing of her own, though, and she wasn't always the timid lamb. Sometimes she was the lioness, daring him to take her…

*****

Sonya, her favorite graduate student and virtual shadow around campus was waiting in Minarra's office when she got back, cross-legged on the couch, poring over a volume of *Plato's Republic* in the original Greek.

"Wow, I can see that went well," she said dryly as Minarra entered the book-cramped space—ever so much smaller than Malcolm's—and slammed the door.

"Mac Macallister is leading the expedition."

Sonya popped her head up from her book. She was somewhere in chapter four, the part about the ideal society. "You don't mean *the* Mac Macallister, do you? Mr. Mummy Hunter and all that from TV?"

"The one and only," she sighed. Minarra had never actually seen any of his television shows. The fact that he had been voted one of the Top 100 Sexiest Men in America by *Hot Shot* magazine was all she needed to know about the level of his current scientific work.

"Oh." As one of her few real friends, Sonya was quite familiar with the Mac saga. "Well doesn't that just restore your faith in the goodness of the universe? Seriously, though, you want me to hold a séance and rustle up some bigger mummies to kick his ass?"

Minarra laughed in spite of herself. It was a typical Sonya remark.

The rail-thin, short-haired ash blonde with a complexion and wardrobe that would put a vampire to shame was a great fan of dark humor. She was also very bad about keeping her hair to a color anywhere near a human shade. Today, by her own account, it was day-glow pink, a hue that had looked bad enough the first time around when it had been used to make peace symbols on sixties protest signs.

"Thank you," Minarra said. "But I'm more than capable of slogging through this one on my own."

Sonya closed the Plato, unconvinced. "You really think you can deal with being around him again, though? After all that happened?"

"I have to don't I? If I want to see Shera-Sa."

Sonya's coal-black eyes narrowed like laser beams. The effect of the younger woman's worry and concern was warming, almost exciting. If Minarra were a lesbian like her, she would no doubt begin a steamy love affair posthaste. "There's something you're not telling me, Priestess."

Minarra winced ever so slightly at the reference to her name. Over her mother's objections, she'd been named after the legendary last high priestess of Shera-Sa who had presided over the city in its final days before being mysteriously swallowed into the desert.

As always, Sonya was reading her with as much ease as that ancient tome on her lap. How was it that Sonya managed to see through her so easily, causing her to lose all her carefully built defense mechanisms?

"I've been having the dreams again," Minarra said.

Sonya pursed her lips. The dreams had been plaguing her off and on for the last month, ever since the mysterious map had surfaced at a bazaar in Madagascar, of all places. An antiquities dealer had found it and, understanding its value, had brought it to the university. It was the first concrete proof of Shera-Sa's existence outside of the legends. Minarra's imagination and spirit had been reborn at the first sight of it. It felt like the greatest blessing of her life to be able to study and understand its inscriptions, but it soon showed a darker side. Just three days after first taking possession of the map, she'd had her first nocturnal experience of the city. And its strange inhabitants.

Chief among them was Komen-tah. The last prince of Shera-Sa, its final blood ruler. Over and over, she would dream of being led to him after being brought into the city by a hooded man in a white robe. The man would take her to the guards in golden breastplates, with swords as clear and sharp as diamonds and shields as round and polished as freshly minted pennies. Stone-faced, they would lead her to the palace and from there to the throne room. She would ask questions, even try to object, but they would never listen.

Sometimes there were others in the throne room—nobles, slave girls, extra guards—sometimes it would be only him. The mysterious prince. Whatever the variation, the man would seek to control her. So far she had managed to escape, running from his golden throne room before he could catch her, but with each dream, she could feel him coming closer to his objective of stripping, chaining and possessing her.

She'd spent a good amount of time lately speculating about what might happen if he ever did. Would it become reality? Would she end up paralyzed, or mad? Was there some black magic in this? Certainly that was one of the legends—that the inhabitants of Shera-Sa had somehow angered the gods with their sorcery and been punished by having their city swallowed whole and the surrounding land turned to desert.

One thing was certain, the prince called her Minarra, as he cried out to her, and the way he looked at her with painful familiarity, gave her the odd feeling that it was the first holder of the name and not her that he was after. But wasn't that just like assuming there was some reality to the dreams, to the prince?

"I know you're still having them," Sonya said. "I've been picking up the vibes all week. But that's not what's bothering you at the moment."

"Go away," Minarra teased, making a cross of her index fingers in front of her. "No telepathic witches allowed."

"You can't get rid of me for at least a decade," she quipped. "You're my thesis advisor, remember?"

"Must you remind me?"

"Yes. I must. Now for the last time, spill the beans or I shall be forced to use my powers to conjure evil spirits to write bad reviews for your next research article."

"Fine. But if I tell you, you promise to leave me be?"

"Witch's honor."

"It's about Mac Macallister." She took a deep breath. "I mean, I do hate him and all…but I'm afraid…"

"Afraid?"

"Yes, afraid." Minarra ran the events of the past hour through her head, ruthlessly analyzing her own behavior. Everything about her strong reactions spelled unresolved emotion. "I think I may still have feelings for him," she confessed.

Sonya grinned. "I knew that, I just wanted to hear you say it."

"Wench."

"You know it," she winked, rising to her feet.

Minarra watched her fish through her purse. A moment later she produced a small, battery-operated vibrator. "Here," she put it on the end of Minarra's desk. "This will help you, while you're figuring out just how much you hate the Mummy Hunter. It's my spare. Mint condition—never used. Money back guarantee if you're not coming like a crazy woman in half an hour."

She sat there for the longest time after Sonya left, just staring at the vibrator. Thoughts were racing through her mind, and sensations too, strong ones. Underneath her skirt, between her legs, below the protective barrier of her cotton panties.

Minarra was moist. Thinking about Mac and his naked body and how he had looked coming toward her in the moonlight. Perfect and shimmering, not an ounce of fat, the muscles perfectly developed, his hair—longer then—swept back over his shoulders like a lion's mane. He was so hard. She hadn't been able to keep her eyes off his cock, though it had made her feel like such a brazen wench.

"It's all right," he'd told her, knowing as always, just the right thing to say. "You're supposed to want to look...and to touch, too."

Minarra licked her suddenly dry lips. Her heart pounding, her arm moving as if of its own accord, she reached across the desk. For the vibrator. For the pleasure she'd denied herself for so very long. Parting her thighs in anticipation, she released a small, jagged sigh.

I'll do it to forget him, she told herself. *To get him out of my system, once and for all.*

It was a good argument, logical even. The trouble was, the heart was not a logical organ. Nor was the pussy. Having this small taste now, would it not want more and more, and eventually the real thing?

Minarra impulsively tossed the thing across the room.

A moment later, she went to retrieve it, inextricably drawn…on her hands and knees…

* * * * *

"Mac, I've no idea what's gotten into her this time," Malcolm fretted as the two men sat alone in the office after Minarra's abrupt departure. "I feel I owe you an apology."

"Not at all," Mac shook his head gravely. "Neither one of you owes me a thing."

If only the kindhearted professor knew how true those words were, Mac thought. There was nothing unwarranted or rude in Minarra's anger. If anything, she'd been too easy on him — given what she'd been through and what she had assumed he'd done to her. It made no difference what his motives had been or his true intent. The bottom line was the same. He'd broken her heart. Shattered it into a million pieces. Nothing left but shards, like ancient artifacts, the desiccated fragments she'd spent her life studying.

Leaving Minarra had been the hardest thing he'd ever had to do in his life. There had been only one thing that could have made him take such a course, and that was the iron will of her father. The inscrutable, unforgiving Roger Hunt.

That morning he had left the camp, an hour before dawn, his clothes in bedrolls, one week's worth of water and gasoline in the spare Rover. He'd been on autopilot. He'd had no desire to live, or even to breathe.

Roger had stood there, a monolith, his sixty-year-old face craggy as a Pharaoh's tomb, his pointed beard sharp as the spear of a Roman legionnaire.

"What can I tell her?" Mac had wanted to know.

Doctor Hunt's usually stony features hardened a notch further. "Go," he pointed toward the horizon. "Don't look back."

Like Lot...threatened with transformation into a pillar of salt. Except Mac had been already dead inside. Funny how no one had noticed that, all these years. He'd been able to remake himself into the perfect adventurer, the perfect enlivener of all that was seemingly dull and arcane in the world of archeology. But for everything he brought to life, he only felt the emptiness that much more in himself.

He'd assumed it was a lifetime sentence. And then had come that incredible, totally unbelievable invitation.

If Minarra thought she was shocked to see him show up here, she ought to have tried being in his shoes the day Malcolm had called asking him to head an expedition to find Shera-Sa. With Minarra Hunt.

Just like old times...

Except there was no Roger this time, to interfere, to keep control. Going over it in his mind, Mac had sometimes wondered if that wasn't part of the thrill. Seducing the daughter of the great and powerful Hunt. The Rasputin of the archeological world. The mad genius who had managed in his day to uncover three new temples and a pyramid. If it hadn't been for his obsession with Shera-Sa, he would have gone down as one of the great scientists of the twentieth century.

As mercurial and possessed as the man was, his only daughter had been beautiful beyond measure. Roger had called her the spitting image of her mother, but Mac thought her even more breathtaking than the woman in the old pictures. It had been love at first sight. Or at least lust. By summer's end, he'd vowed, he would bed the woman, eight years his junior. He'd met his goal a month and a half ahead of schedule. Never had he experienced anything so delicious, so entirely satisfying. Minarra, the shy bookworm, had turned into a tigress in his arms. A writhing cat whom only he could tame. The look in her eyes when finally he would pin her, his hands holding her wrists overhead, the combination of defiance and surrender, wonder and lust—she was all woman. The most purely female being he had ever known.

To this day, he could not be with another, or even enjoy the pleasures of his own flesh without thinking of her. Her face, her body, conjured and superimposed over any other, real or imagined.

He'd hoped that seeing her today would put to rest that old dream. Unfortunately, it had had the opposite effect. One look at her and his pulse had quickened. The blood was pumping from his heart straight to his cock. He'd wanted Minarra, right there in the office. He'd wanted her on the desk, that navy blue skirt up around her waist, her panties down around her ankles, or better still in torn shreds in his hand.

So they couldn't talk anymore, so he'd betrayed her—he still would have fucked her. Would she have objected? Resisted his desires? With her he had never felt a moment's doubt. Her body had belonged to him from the moment he'd seen it. He'd proven it, too, giving her night after night of ecstasy. Mac was no braggart, and he'd be the first to voice any shortcomings with women, but with her, he'd done it right. Five, six orgasms in a session...minimum.

Mac squirmed on the chair. He was having a hard time paying attention to Malcolm. All he could think of was lovely Minarra, on that desk, her legs spread, her gorgeous, naked pink pussy lips fully exposed and ready. Powerless to resist, wanting it as badly as he...

Their bodies slamming together, his shaft fully immersed in her warm heat. That was the only way...to make sense of it all. Or at least to put off the agony of his own failure for a few precious minutes. She'd wrap her ankles around his back...her strong legs... He'd press his chest forward, flattening her breasts. He'd sink his teeth into her neck. She'd hiss at him to get on with it, to complete her conquest, make her come, right there in front of Malcolm. Out of his mind with desire, he'd rear back, pulling as far out as he could without actually withdrawing, and then he'd plunge, for all he was worth, driving her into the desk. She'd cry out her encouragement and he'd do it again. And again. Working up a heat and friction that could set all these old books on fire. Enough combustion to burn down the entire Social Sciences Building. But still, he'd want more, the moans from her soul. And the words. Words of surrender...and devotion.

His mouth, attached to her breast, his semen spurting forth in mind-blowing orgasm, holding her tight and close, for dear life as she bucked and rocked with her own climax...

"Mac, are you quite all right?"

Mac blinked. Malcolm was eying him, his head angled, his brow furrowed.

"Yeah, just some jet lag," he rubbed the back of his head. He was tempted to ask how long he'd been out, daydreaming about making furious love to his supposed colleague.

"I can only imagine, as much traveling as you do."

"It can get wearisome," he admitted. "Listen, Malcolm," he switched gears. "There's something we need to talk about."

Actually, there was quite a lot, but for now there was one pressing concern on his mind.

"You needn't say it," Malcolm sighed. "I can already guess. You are concerned what the effect will be on Minarra if—or more likely when—this mission turns out to be a dead end."

Mac nodded. "Frankly, I'm a little surprised you've managed to get funding."

"It was Minarra's doing. She's a very persistent young woman, as I'm sure you know."

"That's an understatement," he said dryly.

Malcolm chuckled good-naturedly. "I remember when she was about seven. Roger was in Aran-ra. He'd just uncovered the pyramid of Gheeshazar II. Minarra threw a tantrum because she wanted a pyramid of her own. She threatened to run away and dig in the desert with her little shovel until she died of heat exhaustion. Her father finally appeased her by naming the work site after her."

Mac smiled. He'd always soaked up stories about Minarra, trying to fill in the missing pieces of her life in his mind. It was his way of covering the void left by their breakup.

"She wasn't so different the summer I knew her," he observed. "Just a little more grown up."

Malcolm stroked his curly red beard, half gray now, along with his shock of receding Einsteinian hair. "You know, I'll admit, from the few times I saw you two together during my visits to the digs there, I had the impression you might make an interesting pair."

Mac's jaw tensed. "We're oil and water, Malcolm. I just want to make sure she doesn't get hurt. That's why I'm taking this job. Contrary to certain views of me, I am neither a publicity hound nor an ancient UFO chaser. Shera-Sa is dead to me. As dead as the sand out there. What are alive are the Mashutu rebels. Hell, I'm not even sure it'll be safe to take her out of Porto Sayeed, much less go digging around the desert looking for lost cities full of gold."

Malcolm sighed deeply. It was a lot of passion that had just been thrown at him, more than Mac had realized he had inside himself. Could it be there was more here than met the eye? Was it only guilt that had brought him back into Minarra's life to keep her safe, or was it something else?

"Perhaps we oughtn't let her go at all," Malcolm speculated.

Mac shook his head. He wasn't sure of a lot of things in this world, but he knew how Minarra's mind worked. "She'd only find another way, and then we couldn't keep an eye on her. No, it's got to be this way. I'll keep her contained. And if it gets hairy, well, they'll have to kill me to get to her."

"You're a good man," declared Malcolm.

"Not really." Mac was on his feet. "Just one with a lot to atone for. You'll have your expedition. Come hell or high water."

Mac went straight from the archeology office to the restroom. Locking the outer door, he went to the toilet. His cock was hot and hard and pulsing in his hand as he stood over the open bowl. Inside Minarra...he was inside Minarra. Filling and pleasing her, teasing and taking her, making her moan, thrusting to the hilt. Home, after six years of wandering.

Minarra...the rose in the desert. Oasis from which he drank, moist and sweet. The sweet taste of her nipples, her lips, the fragrance of her melting sex. Clenching his eyes tightly, he forced everything but her from his mind. With a single grunt, he released himself, his cock swelling against the pressure of his fingers. His white-hot semen spewed forth. Wasted, fucking wasted. No turning back, he milked it out, running his finger along the vein underneath, soaking up the last bits of pleasure, riding the descending arc, back to ordinary reality.

The act provided him little release, and barely any comfort. If anything, he was angrier now. At himself. At the world. Splashing water on his face, he made the necessary resolutions. He would do his job. He would take Minarra to the desert and cure her once and for all of her foolish obsession. And while he was doing that, god help anyone who tried to harm a hair on her head. Because he would kill them. Without remorse, or mercy or forethought.

* * * * *

Minarra had never done anything like this in her life. Crawling on her hands and knees, in her own office, retrieving a vibrator she had every intention of using. Halfway across the carpeted floor, she thought of turning back, but it was too late. Not with her soaked panties and throbbing nipples, not with the fantasies racing through her mind. It was Mac she imagined doing this for. She was going to let him watch, giving him a show as she played with herself to climax.

The fact that such behavior in real life would be maximally degrading and humiliating seemed somehow to add to the mental thrill. Had she uncovered a streak of masochism in her soul or was she merely trying to prove something to herself—namely that she could get as close as she wanted now to that old Macallister fire and not be hurt again?

Don't fool yourself, said the old ghost, standing over her, hands on his hips. *You're still mine and you always will be. Why do you think you can't be with another man? I own you, Minarra.*

She shook her head. "No," she gasped, though she was thinking *yes* as she snatched up the tiny egg vibrator.

This is a good thing, she told herself. *I'm manipulating him now, using him just how I want, to get off. And by the time I'm done, there will be nothing left of the past.*

Shall I say what you want me to, Minarra? He was naked, the age he was now, and his body just as she knew it would have to be. The ribbed abdomen, the biceps and triceps, perfectly preserved. The only changes were the crow's feet around his eyes and the slight weathering of his skin, the barest concession to gravity and heat and time. *Shall I be your mouthpiece? Your bogeyman puppet? Very well. Lie on your back, then. Spread wide and I'll tell you what you meant to me, the real Mac Macallister.*

Minarra lifted her ass, digging in her heels. Up came the skirt, and down went the panties. She clawed at the material, needing to feel the open air on her bare crotch. She was so ready. So close.

You were a convenient lay, Minarra. How's that for a sweet dark nothing whispered in your ear? I used you, and you let me.

Minarra shivered, touching the vibrating egg against her clit. The sensations were complicated, rich and contradictory. Just like her thoughts. She wanted this and she didn't, and that made her want it more than anything in her whole life.

That's it. Show me what a female is good for. I got all I wanted from you and I moved on, and now I'm going to use you all over again. You like this, bare-assed on your carpet? Behaving like some kind of little tramp?

Minarra reached for her breast, grasping at the nipple beneath her blouse. She pinched it. Hard. Mac was laughing in the background. Taunting her.

This is all you'll get. Not my body. No matter how much you beg. Though you're welcome to try. You always were a good little beggar, weren't you?

Minarra arched her back, waves of shame pouring over her, white-hot and deliciously deep. Where was it all coming from? She'd barely had any sexual drive at all in years. "Going to...come..." she grunted softly, as though she were not alone.

Go ahead, that's why I'm here.

The smooth, rounded surface of the egg was shaking her to the core. Her clit was swollen like a tiny cock. Her sex was gaping, the walls of her vagina spasming as though the man were thrusting in her hole, even now. Every muscle in her body tensed and released, pulsed, like electricity racing up and down her spine. She wanted to tear off the rest of her clothes, she wanted to throw open her door, she wanted the rest of the world to see.

Freedom...an end to all these years of dark loneliness, of being frozen inside, her only dream that of a city full of ghosts, older than mummies, a thousand years before the time of the Pyramids. A city of which she dreamed, and in which there was a man who wanted her. Very badly.

Minarra had to put her hand over her mouth. Her hips were gyrating, rocking, moving in rhythm with the orgasm. It wasn't just one orgasm, but three, rising peaks, one after the other. So much pent-up energy, so much latent desire. Hands on her body...mouths on her skin. Cocks filling her...

Her breath rose to panting. Now she imagined herself in that throne room of her dream with the mysterious Prince Komen-tah. He was naked, his bronzed body the envy of any god, his erect cock a scepter to be worshipped by the alabaster maidens fawning at his feet. There were young men, too, the makings of an orgy, laughing and dancing amidst the stories high, marble-columned, silver-domed chamber, grapes being dipped into tipped back mouths, wine pouring into throats and bodies being handed about amongst the highborn elders, the sexy slaves writhing on the golden floor.

Minarra groaned. The details—how would she know such things that went beyond the scholars' records? How could she create this? The smell of incense and liquid lust, the heat of flaring nostrils, the bull god statues lining the walls, breathing the air, the distant blare of trumpets and the roll of drums, like thunder. An empire such as the world has never known again, all congealed in a single moan...

It was so real, as though it was the fantasy having her and not the other way around...

Greedily, craving more, Minarra kept the vibrator in place for yet another climax, raising the stakes, causing the sweat to bead on her skin, the blood rising to the surface, hot to the touch. She was Icarus, flying up to the sun. She cried out, but no sounds came from her throat.

She thought she could hear the sound of male laughter…more than human. *Komen-tah, is that you?*

Some minutes later—or was it hours—she opened her eyes and attempted to move. She was still alive and Mac's ghost was definitely gone from the room, along with the bogeymen she kept conjuring from Shera-Sa. It was time to go back to work, she sighed. Time to stop all this emotional nonsense. If there was one thing she would not be it was what her father called a "hysterical woman". By which he meant any woman who did not behave precisely as would a man.

There were a million things to do. Months of research to complete in one week. And scads of packing. Just making the list would take an hour or more. At the top of that list would be ignoring Mac Macallister to whatever extent she could manage. She would neither hate nor love him. She would not even acknowledge his existence, save the bare minimum required to plan and execute the expedition. He'd be an object, a neutral component and nothing more.

Her emotions might balk a little, but it was a matter of simple discipline. Prioritization, execution and follow-through. That's what her daddy had always said. This mission would be for him. And once it was over, regardless of the outcome, she would walk away from Mac Macallister, cured forever of her pain.

Chapter Two

Minarra's plan to avoid Mac worked well over the next week. She kept busy, translating the map, preparing the necessary materials. Sonya chided her for not stopping to eat and sleep, but frankly she did not want the time to either think or dream. There'd be time for that later, after she got back home, after the research results were all tabulated and she'd written her landmark book. She could take a nice sabbatical and laze around a cabin in the mountains.

The map translation went well. There was a code employed in the legend and designations, based on a variation of binary numeration. Employing the template, she could make a pretty good guess where Shera-Sa would have been.

Where it was, still.

The value of the map alone could not be underestimated. The binary code was also matched to a reference grid on the reverse side, which showed equivalency symbols in Egyptian hieroglyphics as well as in the Sumerian alphabet. It was the closest anyone had come yet to providing proof that the Near Eastern civilizations had a common ancestor.

Had she wished, she might have made a career of this study alone. But that was not her purpose in life. Her father had left her his own legacy, the much bigger mantle of finding the ruins of the proto-civilization itself.

No one had ever been closer. She wished he could have lived to see it. Her only hope was that she would live up to his expectations. That she would be hardheaded, rational and iron-willed. As he would have been.

Minarra's confidence rose to a peak as she boarded the airplane. Mac had been back in her life for a week now and she'd withstood him like iron. It was like a test, a dry run for the mission itself, and she was virtually certain she could handle anything that the man might throw at her.

She was done with him emotionally. Really done.

What she hadn't banked on, however, was having him as her seatmate on the plane ride to Alcazara. Twice she looked at her ticket, frowning. "There must be some mistake," she said icily, noting his occupation of the first class window seat next to hers on the aisle.

"Is there?" Mac pulled his own ticket from the inner pocket of his tweed jacket. He was wearing an oxford shirt, his body freshly scrubbed and smelling of musk. She gripped the edge of the seat, her knees dangerously weakened. The sight of him, mildly dressed up, all that masculine power and energy thinly disguised under a veneer of polite society had always done something to her insides, something that could only be resolved with hot kisses, with her hands fervently trying to unbutton, her eyes begging attention…conquest.

She wasn't the only woman he had this effect on. Be it a roomful of high society types or a class full of coeds hearing one of his "awesome" lectures, Mac Macallister reduced them all to elemental females, on display, estrogen surging.

What made him most hot was that he wasn't trying to impress. He kept himself in tiptop shape for his own reasons, and he kept his own agenda and goals. She'd seen that this week, watching him interact with the students, teachers and staff at the university. It was the same old Mac—and yet he seemed sadder, somehow. Weighed down...

"No. I believe I have the right seat. See for yourself."

Her nostrils flared at the scent of him as he raised his arm. The musk was mixed with a clean, soapy smell. A man smell. It made her want to nuzzle and snuggle and touch...

There was no way she'd make it all the way to freaking North Africa like this.

"That won't be necessary," she refused his invitation to inspect his ticket. "I'm sure you're right. I'll just switch with someone else."

"Suit yourself."

Minarra gritted her teeth. Suit herself? The nerve of the man. He was the one who'd wronged her—he should be getting up. Apologizing for taking up part of her row, for breathing her air, for daring to still be on the same planet.

"Is something wrong, Minarra?"

The man was messing with her head. He had to be. Well she'd be damned if she'd turn tail and run. Let him be the one to sit and squirm across the Atlantic.

"Not a thing," she smiled broadly, plopping herself down. "I'm as happy as a lark."

He cast her a puzzled look, pure male. "If you say so."

"I do," she said icily. "And I'd appreciate it if we passed this trip in silence."

Mac shrugged and took out a pair of reading glasses. They didn't suit him somehow. Too academic, maybe? Three times in the next half hour she complained about the noise he was making with his newspaper, though honestly, a mouse could not have been quieter.

Feeling cranky and tired as hell, Minarra refused her dinner of filet mignon in favor of a pillow and a sleep mask. Taking off her shoes, she curled her skirt-clad legs underneath her, turned to her side—away from Mac—and went to sleep.

* * * * *

Mac had never felt so perplexed in his life. He knew he ought to have done something. But what? Would she have been insulted if he'd offered to change seats? Was it better to just play it cool by staying put? And why in hell couldn't he bring himself to talk to her like he'd been wanting to.

There was so much he wanted to explain. But the emotions just got crammed up in his head. The way they'd been doing for all these years. His fans called him brave, for daring to break into cursed tombs and search hostile jungles for lost artifacts. In truth he was a coward when it came to the most important thing in his life.

Hiding behind a newspaper only made it worse. And every time she barked at him, he only felt more like a complete cad. He should have anticipated this might happen. As expedition leader, he ought to have personally arranged the seats, so she wouldn't have to sit with him. Now it was too awkward for either one of them to change without tipping off the others that there was something between them.

Dinner was a welcome break. So was her decision to go to sleep. The steak was delicious, and he devoured it, ravenous. It was dark by the time he'd finished and he was more than happy to turn down the lights for a quiet rest. The sounds of the cabin were relatively calming, and he was hopeful he might get a little sleep himself. He knew he would have to hit the ground running when they landed in Alcazara.

They would go by bus from the airport to Porto Sayeed, the sprawling, thief-infested coastal city through which flowed most of the goods, legal and illegal for this rough and violent desert country. It would be his responsibility to hire guides, and extra gunmen, in the event of trouble. He would also negotiate for supplies. Camels, water and other basics. The main challenge, beyond avoiding getting his throat slit, would be to keep the ever curious and feisty Minarra out of harm's way.

She seemed innocent enough asleep. Leaning across, he flicked an errant curl back from where it had strayed over her eyelid. This small, beautiful woman had always managed to trigger such emotions in him. Protectiveness. Jealousy. And at times, rage. It was an incident involving such passion that had led indirectly to his banishment from Hunt's summer digs at Maleeka. Because of her father's strict rules about fraternization, not to mention his fierce feelings of possessiveness toward his daughter, they had kept their affair a secret. The need to do so had fueled their young passion and allowed them to play all manner of sexy and dangerous games.

One time, for example, he'd fucked her from behind in broad daylight, sneaking up on her while she'd stood hanging clothes on the line to dry.

"Just act natural," he'd pulled her shorts and panties down to the bottom of her ass.

"Mac, don't," she'd pleaded.

Mac had found her wet and receptive. She was always that way for him. Without exception. "Why not?" he'd teased, plunging his cock deep inside her. "I'm just exercising my property rights."

She'd melted against him, her breath ragged. It was a big turn-on for both of them when he talked this way, about ownership and control. Over and over she'd ask for stories—what did he know about the female slaves he'd seen and what did it feel like to touch a brand on a woman's thigh?

Minarra was far from a slave herself, though. She enjoyed teasing him, especially if it made him want her all the more. What Minarra didn't understand was how the minds of other men worked. More than one of the workers saw her confidence, her blossoming sexuality. The new attention she was getting seemed innocent enough to her, but Mac knew better. Especially when it had come to Kalid. On more than one occasion he'd seen the man watching her across the dining tent, his dark eyes hungrily studying her in her shorts and tank tops, the way her body naturally moved, so spunky and sensual, so deliciously female. Her moves and her bright smiles had been for him, but Kalid had thought he could cash in.

He'd thought wrong.

Mac'd had a little man-to-man talk with him late one night, behind the latrine. With a few simple words, the man's back pushed against the wooden wall, Mac had made his case clear.

If he ever got wind of Kalid so much as looking at her funny again, he'd cut his balls off and feed them to the camels. Kalid was a muscular man, but he'd had no stomach to fight the American. Instead he'd gone straight to Roger and told him that Mac was screwing his daughter. The irony was that Kalid hadn't even known this for a fact—he'd been merely trying to hurt Mac with a lie.

Roger had looked into the matter, quickly realizing he'd had his head in the sand about a lot of things. Calling Mac into his tent the next night, he'd dropped the bomb.

"My daughter will never marry anyone like us. I won't allow it. You can either leave now, quietly, or I will have you removed."

Mac hadn't bothered telling Roger that he hadn't even thought of marrying Minarra. Under the circumstances, that would only have added insult to injury. "I'll go," he'd said, adding, "Roger, I'm sorry, I never meant to hurt anyone."

Roger had gone back to his book, his gaunt face eerily lit by the lantern hanging from the center pole. It had been a clear message that the meeting was at an end.

The next morning, loaded down with supplies, he had made his getaway, his feet as heavy as lead, his soul as empty as the desert stretched out before him.

* * * * *

The bronze-skinned Komen-tah had chained her naked, arms stretched between two columns. Stripped nude, his amber-green eyes glowing like Egyptian jewels, his smile like an asp, quick and deadly, he approached her, a long, black, braided whip in his hands. Minarra struggled, but she was no match for the chains.

The golden throne room was full of laughing slave girls, in scraps of sequined silk, reclining on plush red cushions. They wore anklets of steel and collars around their necks.

"Prophesy to me, my Minar-ra," proclaimed Komen-tah. His head was shaved bald this time, save for a long ponytail of braided, raven's wing hair. He wore a necklace of gold, set with splendid gems, many of them colors and varieties she had never seen before. She had the distinct sense they served some purpose, almost like controls to an unseen mechanism. His face was painted this time, with razor thin black lines on the side of each eye and red tear drops on each cheek.

"Stay away from me," she cried.

"Minar-ra," he soothed, touching her chin, once again using the Shera-Sa pronunciation of her name. "My lovely priestess. Why will you not worship me?"

So this was it. This last prince of Shera-Sa was mad. He thought himself to be the creator of the universe, not a mere kingly god, but god above all gods. Did this have something to do with the city's destruction?

"I'm not her," said Minarra. "And you aren't real. You're just a ghost."

The robust Komen-tah turned to the slave girls, encouraging their boisterous response. "Did you hear that? I am not real," he told them. "And neither, therefore, is this."

They squealed as he held his erect cock in his hand. Komen-tah's phallus was enormous, thick and banded with green circular designs. One by one they fell to the floor, on their bellies, begging to be fucked. He spurned them all.

"They seem to think me real enough, Priestess. Shall we test the hypothesis?" Prince Komen-tah's body touched hers, hot as fire. He was a huge man, a wall of muscle, inescapable. The more she squirmed, the more she accommodated his hot desire.

"Please," she cried in vain.

He slid the coiled whip down her left side. "You will perform for me, Priestess. You will give me pleasure watching you writhe under the whip. Such will be my victory over the gods. I shall humble them, through you. And when the whipping is done, you will service me. I've a new sacrament for you…and it involves swallowing."

"No," she shook her head desperately.

Pushing his cock into her belly button he grabbed the back of her neck for a kiss. It was deep and rude, but arousing nonetheless. Smashing her defenses, he slipped down, into her consciousness, making her want and need all the wicked things he planned to do. Her pussy dripped in reply and she began to pant. Shame racked her body as the slaves commented on the easiness of her response, the way she welcomed the cruel treatment.

He released her, a shattered woman. "I believe you were saying something? What was it?" he asked amused. "Oh yes, I believe it was no."

She groaned as he laid the whip coil against the opening to her sex. He was grazing her clit, forcing her to feel unwanted pleasure with every breath.

"Is it still your intent to defy me?" he wanted to know.

Minarra shook her head no.

He smiled in triumph. "In that case," his eyes bore into hers. "You may come for me…"

She began to spasm, the fluids pouring out of her in floods. The entire room was being filled. They were all going to drown. The slave girls screamed as one by one they were washed away. Minarra fought like mad to get away, but Komen-tah was holding her, keeping her in place. The shouts for help coming from her mouth were not penetrating the water. She was going to die.

At the last second, she heard Mac's voice. She was in his arms, and he was pulling her up and out of danger…

* * * * *

Mac was just lulling off into a semiconscious state when he heard Minarra cry out. She was having a bad dream, softly moaning, fighting something off. Instinctively, he gathered her in his arms.

"Honey, it's all right. You're safe." Time evaporated, the breakup was a thing of the past, or was it the future? He'd been down this road before. Minarra had always had nightmares, though she would seldom remember the experiences the next morning.

"I have to…escape…the flood…" she was saying.

"Min, you're dreaming." He leaned her back, taking her face in his hands, one palm on either cheek. "You feel that? It's reality. Wake up and feel what's real."

Her breathing slowed after a couple of more gasps. At last her eyes opened, slowly. "M-Mac?"

He hadn't intended to kiss her. Really it was the worst thing in the world he could have done, but there'd been no way to squelch his instincts in time. Those bright, beautiful eyes of hers lit up for a moment and then her lids slid dreamily closed. The hands that a moment ago had pushed at his chest now reached around his neck, drawing him close.

Mac's erection rose to meet her. If it could have, his cock would have opened the zipper by itself.

Oh god, he needed Minarra…but on an airplane? Three rows back from the pilot? Covering her with the blanket bought him time to think. So did sliding his hand up under the hem of her skirt. He drew a breath, quick and sharp at the firm, familiar silkiness. Those legs. Her thighs. She hadn't lost a bit of her assets.

"Nnnn, Mac." Her teeth were chattering. She had her head back, her neck arched, and she was holding his wrist. Was she trying to get his hand off her body or did she want it higher, closer to her center?

He worked his way under the side panel of her panties. He was nearly at the point of no return. "Tell me to stop, Min. Or not."

"Just take me," she thrashed her head. "You know you will anyway."

"No, Min, it's your choice," he said fiercely.

"I don't want a fucking choice, Mac. I'll only feel shittier about this when it's over."

Fuck. Talk about making a man feel like a heel…

"Forget it," he growled. "This is a mistake."

Minarra pushed him away. There was something wild in her eyes, something he'd never seen before. With hair all disheveled like this and her lips puffy from sleep, she looked like some kind of succubus, pure *eros*, pure darkness.

"I'll be in the bathroom," she told him. "I need some air."

He refrained from grabbing her. More than anything he wanted to follow her, the sway of that ass and the motion of those flanks. He was having visions of her, pinned against the wall of the tiny restroom, her palms on the metal, his cock slipping into her from behind. Screwing like rabbits at fifty-thousand feet.

Talk about crazy. For one thing, there were all the new security regulations. Only one person in the toilet at a time. Granted, he could sneak in, but still, it would be opening a Pandora's Box. Reopening a nearly fatal wound for the sake of a quickie…a total violation of every rule of sane and healthy human conduct.

He had to laugh at that one.

As if their passion had ever followed any rules.

What exactly is that you're lying on? He'd asked her the day she'd surprised him, naked in his tent, happily arrayed on a Persian rug.

You know damned well what it is, she'd propped her chin up on her hands, her knees bent behind her as she lay on her belly. *It's a priceless Khartoush Dynasty Coronation rug.*

The one from your father's tent?

What do you think? They have these lying around at the bazaar in town?

You're fucking crazy.

Nope. Just fucking horny.

It killed him to think what he'd done to that playful, impish young woman—totally destroying the trust she'd so fully placed in him. Like a bird, spreading its wings in the wrong palm, only to have them crushed.

There was no way he could go after her now. It would be taking advantage. She wasn't fully awake. That look in her eyes—whatever she'd dreamt this time had messed with her head. Her mother Sofia had had the dreams, too. Roger had told him. They got worse just before the insanity kicked in. From there it was all downhill…

Fear gripped Mac's heart as he thought of Sofia's end. Discovered early one morning, an empty bottle of pills in her hand. He couldn't leave Minarra alone right now, as much as he knew it was wrong to pursue her for sex. He'd go just to talk to her, to get her back to her seat so she could share what had happened and let him help her work through it.

Helping—that was it. Not sex. No matter how badly he wanted it. And her.

* * * * *

Minarra slid the latch to the occupied position, not daring to breathe until she was securely within the confines of the steel compartment. It had been a close call, far too close for comfort. She'd very nearly succumbed to him, despite all of her resolve and carefully built walls of hatred and loathing.

The dream was responsible. That accursed, mind-eating, repetitive dream.

She had opened her eyes and seen his face, full of concern, so strong and masculine, yet so tender. She'd called his name and then…they were kissing.

Things had gotten fuzzy again. He'd touched her and she'd responded, but something had held them back and the next thing she knew she was running away.

She'd made good her escape. The question was, *now what*?

She splashed water on her face. She was shaking all over. What was happening to her? Her reflection in the mirror showed a woman she barely recognized. Between the stress and lack of sleep, the pressure of getting this mission ready while dealing with all these dreams, she had been gradually wearing herself to a frazzle.

But there was something else, too—a different glint in her eyes, ancient and fierce and alien. Almost like someone else staring back at her. Was it her imagination fired by all her readings, or was she quite possibly looking at some facet of the Minar-ra of old?

"Minarra. Open up." It was Mac, knocking on the door.

"Go away."

"No, I won't. Let me in now, or I'll break the door down."

"Don't be crazy. The pilot or someone will shoot you."

"I'll take the chance. I'm not kidding, Minarra, let me in."

Minarra uttered a curse under her breath. He was just crazy enough to do something like that, too. She slid the latch to unoccupied. He turned the handle at once, opening the door.

The room was filled with his presence. Tall and strong. And comforting. The last thing she wanted to do was bury her head against his chest...but that's exactly what was happening. The way his arms wrapped around her, so tight and perfect, both comforted and alarmed her.

They were too good of a fit. Always had been.

"Min, tell me what's going on?"

She looked up into his eyes. Kissing him was a cheat, a way to avoid the subject—along with all the others between them. He did not refuse. He was a man, after all. He tasted of fresh mouthwash. A bit of stubble brushed her cheek. Suddenly nothing mattered but him. He absorbed her senses, her essence.

Here was an opportunity, she thought, her mind working in split second flashes, to drive away the loneliness, to silence the pain and doubts.

Minarra pulled him back, so she was pinned against the wall. Grabbing him by the collar, she made it clear in no uncertain terms.

"Fuck me."

He was hesitating, despite his obvious arousal. So the bastard was trying to be all moral on her now?

"Fuck me," she repeated, hissing the vulgarity as she went to work on his zipper. "You owe me that much."

His face darkened—he wasn't happy with what she was saying, but that was his tough luck. He had taken things this far, he'd stacked the deck from day one of their relationship, so he'd bloody well come through now when she was horny and scared.

He sealed the bathroom door with his palm and locked it. "You've changed," he pulled up her skirt. "You're...different."

"I'm not that naïve young woman anymore," she agreed, exposing his cock—that magnificent spear she knew so well. The man had lost nothing of his virility. It was every bit as hard and sensitive and pulsing as she remembered. Touching the vein underneath, the part she knew drove him wild, she added. "So you'd better live up to my standards."

The frown was visible. She'd hit a nerve. "How many others have there been, Min?"

She laughed, enjoying the pain she seemed to be causing. "I don't keep count, sweetheart. Do you?"

"There are things you don't understand." He pulled her skirt up, out of the way. Those creamy, white thighs, the delta under those sweet, cotton panties, and that ass of hers, a perfect heart. The way she was acting he wasn't sure if he wanted to fuck her or spank her.

"Oh I'm sure. A man has needs…he can't be tied down… Just out of curiosity, how many others were you screwing at the same time as me? Iona? She had the big tits remember? What about Helga? A little old, but hey, I guess any hole will do."

The sarcasm wasn't lost. "Don't be hurtful, Min. I told you, you don't understand…"

"I don't have to," she wriggled her panties down, with the direct aim of matching up his cock to her moist opening underneath. "I'm just a piece of ass. Same now as then. Daddy told me how you handle women."

The words were like a blow to the solar plexus. He'd been half-afraid Roger would cover things with lies, but he hadn't wanted to believe his mentor capable of such a thing. "What did Roger tell you?"

"Just the truth, big boy. Now stop talking and fuck me. You don't deserve a conversation."

Mac scooped her up by her ass cheeks and impaled her, his uncircumcised cock head easily parting her swollen, pink lips. She was more than ready, lubricated and inviting.

"It's not that easy. Not by a long shot." Working his length in and out a couple of times, he lifted her legs, helping her to wrap them around his ass. Her sharp words quickly changed to soft moans and whimpers. She laid her head on his shoulder, her fingers clutching at his back. Her breath was ragged, every tiny motion of her lungs bringing her to what he knew from experience was the edge of orgasm.

She was so fucking beautiful like this, so completely vulnerable, yet filled with a fire that could incinerate half a city. It was he who had helped her make that discovery in herself. The buried riches of her own sex. His name belonged on that find. There was no way another man could go there and do that. There was no way she could respond like that with anyone else.

The very thought of it drove him out of his mind…

"How many?" He asked again compulsively, employing a single, powerful thrust. "How many have you let get inside you…after all we had?"

God — what am I saying? What sense did that make? He'd spent the first two years after the breakup filling his life with empty sex to dull the pain, and she hadn't even had the benefit of knowing why the thing had happened at all.

"How many, Min? Five? Ten? Fifty?" He couldn't help himself. He'd gone too far already. It was a jealousy fuck now. "You will tell me, if I have to make you name them all."

"None," she cried, spasming around his cock, her drenched, molten pussy clenching and unclenching in orgasmic fury. "Not a single…fucking…one. Are you happy, asshole?"

Mac came amid a swirl of emotions. Guilt and shame and pity for himself, yet also a kind of deep, male satisfaction. So Minarra was still his woman, in a very real sense. She'd never gone to another for comfort. She'd never let another claim her body.

He grunted, like a man stabbed, squeezing out every last drop, filling her. *His* woman... She'd waited six years, more gorgeous than ever, free spirited, untamed, except by him. And now here he was, back again—enjoying the best sex in all that time, feeling better than he had in years. It was all so very simple. Just a nice, neat little do-over and go on, right?

Except there'd be a lot of questions, wouldn't there? Like why, even if he did leave her out of respect for her father, didn't he come back for her after the old man's death less than a year later? Why had he stood, watching her from afar, at the funeral? In her black dress she had looked so elegant and lovely, so tortured and frail. Why hadn't he held her then, instead of waiting until now—in an airplane bathroom?

He couldn't answer that. He only knew that he had not belonged at that funeral, nor, at that point, in her life at all. He'd skulked away from the graveside, across the green lawns, back to his jeep, leaving Minarra by the granite headstones of Sofia and Roger Hunt.

"Minarra," he breathed in the wake of the storm, the rushing air of the vents partially obliterating his plea. "I'm sorry...for all of it."

She shoved him away, as far as the tight quarters would allow. "Leave me alone, Mac. Go, now."

He stuffed his cock back in his pants. There was no way he'd touch all those emotions...like a pile of coiled snakes, slithering and hissing. "All right, Min, have it your way."

She locked the door again after him. He could hear the sound of crying as he walked back to his seat.

A few minutes later she came out, fully composed. Resuming her seat, waiting for him to rest his head and nod off against the window of the airplane, she said, "And just so you know, nothing is going to change. I am not going to jump willy-nilly into your arms now. In fact, I am not even going to treat you as a civilized human being, except where absolutely vital to this expedition."

He attempted a small olive branch. "I'm glad at least we'll still be working together."

The answer seemed to irritate her. "Don't play coy, I know what you were up to, and it didn't work in there. You thought you'd use me? Well I used you. How does it feel, big man? I got off on you. I used you for your cock."

"I don't think you believe that, Minarra."

"Fuck you," she told him. And that was the last thing she said until the plane landed.

Chapter Three

In order to stay calm, focused and rational, Minarra diverted herself, making a thorough study of everything in her environment on the way to the hotel. Porto Sayeed was a place of stark and terrible contrasts. From the window of the rickety double-decker vehicle, she could observe, on this particular street, a row of stick supported canopies, a bazaar, teeming with long-robed merchants offering everything from figs to Fujika cameras. An old woman in a veil selling woven prayer rugs sat quietly next to a young man in a USA T-shirt hawking CD players. Tinny, Arabian music played from loudspeakers on wooden poles, interspersed with the live flute of a snake charmer and the sounds of rap music coming from a boom box. Children played something akin to jacks on the cobblestone street, as armed soldiers watched warily, machine guns at the ready.

They'd been traveling downhill, following the general contours of the city that led to the harbor, the mouth of Porto Sayeed, in more ways than one. Pirates had a different slang for the opening through which they thrust their vessels, one the priests and mullahs would hardly approve. Minarra found it interesting herself. That this same, teeming, self-contradictory haven for the tall ships traveling over crystal-blue seas, could be synonymous with sex, worship, commerce, or in the case of some souls, sheer magic.

Prisoner of Shera-Sa

In the same way, she could choose to regard what happened with Mac in any number of ways. The proper thing to do was to assign it as little value as possible. The same with the dreams. They were as real and deep as she made them. Granted, she was becoming a bit hesitant to sleep...but that didn't mean there was anything real behind them.

Much of what she was seeing today was familiar from her childhood—minus the high-tech soldiers and rap music. Her father had spent a good many summers here compiling his research. To her, these bazaars had been a magical place, the land of Aladdin come alive, a thousand colors and sights and sounds and smells. The danger had been little then, and she'd often gone about on her own, striking cunning deals with the merchants for small trinkets and pieces of juicy fruit, fighting imaginary pirates and swooning over imaginary princes under the golden-red sunset.

She now looked for the bigger picture, past the nearby rooftops. In the distance she could make out the towers of the minarets, next to the saw-toothed edges of old crusader castles. Above, the sky was an incredible, pure blue, ancient as the Bible, fresh as the pomegranates overflowing from the baskets of the women riding the bus with them. It was a local bus, half-filled with women traveling to the bazaar, as well as some schoolchildren and a few civil servant types in old, threadbare suits, matched with head coverings. It was late afternoon by now, the end of the midday siesta, a habit adopted from the brief period of Spanish rule here, prior to that of the French and then the British.

The smells were themselves a complicated feast, as varied as the styles and ethnic origin of the people in the streets. The odor of goats and camels was a piquant overlay to the delicious piquancy of curry-like spices and the warm, deep undercurrent of the various pita breads, cooked meats and rich espressos from the cafes.

Minarra didn't realize until now just how hungry she was. She'd stubbornly refused food on the airplane, and again at the airport. It was Mac's fault, for acting so pompously, lecturing her about needing to keep her strength up.

"I'll be just fine," she'd snapped. "Go work out your guilt on someone else."

It was terribly unprofessional of her, not to mention childish. She was stuck, now, though, at least until they got to the hotel.

They had begun this journey from the airport in a taxi. A four-decades-old European limo peppered with dents and bullet holes, and for some inexplicable reason, the driver had refused to take them into the bounds of the city itself.

Mac had mumbled something about a strike when she asked why he was behaving so strangely, but it was clear the man knew more than he was saying. That pissed her off, too. They were supposed to be colleagues. She was not a child.

"We'll argue later," he'd said, steering her by the arm onto the nearby bus, allowing the taxi driver to keep their luggage. The one thing she took was the small gray attaché, the one with her wallet, passport and, of course, the map to Shera-Sa.

She hadn't missed the fact that he was wearing his sidearm or that he had had them both change into khakis at the small, sweltering terminal of Aero Alcazara. Picking up what she could from the people in line at customs — she was as fluent as Mac in the local language and dialects — it seemed the security situation was worsening. Westerners, prime targets of the rebels, were particularly unwanted.

Perhaps that explained the driver's hesitancy. He did not wish to be seen in the city shuttling foreigners. It would be nice if Mac had consulted her, however, on how they were going to deal with each eventuality.

The bus stopped at the main terminal, a hodgepodge station whose architecture was a cross between the onion-domed Kremlin and an airplane hanger.

"Stick by my side," he said as soon as they'd climbed down the wooden slat stairs onto the concrete platform. "I'll do all the talking from here on in. Just keep your eyes low, follow my commands."

Minarra glared. She should have seen this coming...a complete testosterone *coup d'état*. It never failed when guys got in an Old World country like this. Well, Mac Macallister was about to be reminded that she was not an Old World woman.

"Gee," she smiled acerbically. "Did I miss something? She felt her bare neck and then patted her ass. "No...I don't feel a collar or a tail. So I guess I'm not your little fucking pet then, huh?"

He drew a breath, as if she were the one behaving foolishly. "Minarra, this isn't the time or place. Things are unfolding here fast — faster than I had expected. This is not the Alcazara you remember where archeologists' little girls get to eat in the palace with the king and wear the jewels of princesses around their necks."

Minarra's blood moved quickly past the point of boiling. "How dare you," she accused. "That was a precious memory I shared with you once and now you take it and use it as a weapon? Of course I know it's not the eighties anymore, you asshole. King Salaam—my father's dear friend was assassinated a decade ago. I was seventeen at the time…already way past the illusions of childhood."

Mac frowned. "I'm sorry, Min. I didn't mean it like that. I'm just trying to protect you. Outspoken women, especially white ones are not nearly as tolerated anymore. The more you appear subservient, the safer we will both be."

She turned up her nose. "That's your opinion. I intend to find out for myself. I've done research. There is a strong democracy movement here too, and—"

Mac released a frustrated male sigh. "Damn it, woman, must you be so completely pigheaded about everything?"

She shook out her hair defiantly, determined to stand her ground, yet oddly relieved at the same time not to have to be all on her own here, making all her own choices and standing against whatever enemies might be out there. "Excuse me for trying to hold a civilized discussion," she retorted.

If only they could reach some sort of compromise. Then again, that assumed the man was anything more than a thoughtless barbarian.

A barbarian who's trying to protect me, she thought, operating from that secret, treasonous, "alpha male adoring" part of herself. *A man who cares enough to get angry and is not afraid to be strong when he needs to…*

A woman could fall for a man like that. She could dare to open the softest, most feminine side of herself.

Offering, surrendering, as completely as any local harem girl. But wait, she'd already done that. And been burned to a crisp.

Mac took her wrist. "I'm not a civilized human being...remember?"

"This is kidnapping," she informed him as he marched her down the street.

"I'm just doing my job. Keeping you safe...from yourself."

The Hotel Sayeed was two blocks from the station. In its heyday it had hosted the rich and famous from all over Europe, including the royal families of several countries. These days it was occupied by businessmen—the few still willing to work deals with an increasingly unreliable government. Since the king's death, a series of ineffectual caretakers had followed. The most recent, Hassan VIII, was the worst of all.

It was a sandstone structure, ten stories high, with ornate copper grillwork and columns. The doormen still wore long red coats and pith helmets, in the old British style. Three of them were on hand to let Mac and Minarra inside the lobby. No questions were asked at to their lack of a vehicle or luggage. Mac paused to give the head man an Alcazaran fifty-pound note, thanking him for his service, which confirmed Minarra's suspicions that the taxi driver had already been by with their bags.

Once inside, he switched to holding her hand, though his grip was no-nonsense. She blushed a bit at the assumption others would make—namely that they were lovers. There were few people about. An old man with a goatee, in a white suit and a wide-brimmed hat sat in a high-backed wicker chair reading a paper while a barefoot boy in rags polished his shiny black shoes. Two women in smart business suits were quietly conversing near the elevator with a white-robed man who looked like some sort of sheik.

The marble lobby was as elegant as Minarra had remembered. Huge fans hung from the ceiling, their brass blades decorated in gold. Vases, the envy of any palace, stood guard at every doorway. The reception desk was of polished teak and the paneling on the walls was mahogany. The cigar smoke, rising in lazy wisps from the old man's mouth, was pure *Cubano*.

"*Shelem vakim*, my American friend." The white-gloved manager bowed crisply.

"*Vakim shelem*, Osiron," replied Mac, returning the greeting. "You are looking well. The wives must be feeding you extra portions." He teased in Alcazaran.

"Actually," said the man in English, perfect and neatly clipped. "I blame the mistresses. But you are being rude," he chided, passing him the register to sign. "You have neglected to introduce this radiant flower whose beauty you are clearly unworthy of."

"This is Minarra," he supplied. "My fiancée."

"Your fiancée! Ah, my dear child," the sleek dark-haired, dark-skinned man lamented. "You have my sympathies. And you—" He waved his finger at Mac. "You ought to be on your knees thanking the gods for such undeserved fortune."

"I do so, every night before bed, don't I, darling?"

Minarra squeezed Mac's hand to the bone by way of response, indicating just how amused she was by this little charade of his. He'd pay for this later, when she got him behind closed doors. This and all the rest of it.

The manager laughed, his pencil-thin mustache vibrating ever so slightly. "Be careful, my friend, Allah does not like liars. Does he, dear lady?"

"No, he doesn't," Minarra agreed, deciding she liked this Osiron almost as much she hated Mac. "He certainly does not."

"I shall need to repent," Mac smiled behind his wince.

Good. She was getting to him.

"So shall we all." The manager's eyebrow rose ever so slightly, indicating something, or someone over his left shoulder.

Mac nodded in reply. The exchange had been almost imperceptible. She bided her time through the rest of the small talk. In a few moments, Mac was leading her to the elevator. She spotted the man they had referred to before. He was dressed in coveralls, holding a screwdriver, attending to one of the brass fixtures mounted on the wall.

Obviously he was some sort of spy. But for whom? This whole situation had way more questions than answers. Supposedly they were here to round up their guide and the rest of the team, collect their supplies and head into the desert. To this point, however, it was more like a Tom Clancy novel.

Minarra's bags were waiting in the Oasis suite, along with Mac's small valise. He opened the bag, moved aside some colored T-shirts and pulled out a spare clip for his forty-five-caliber pistol. "You'll wait here," he slipped the dark, metal piece into his pocket. "While I make the final arrangements with our guides."

"The hell I will," she declared defiantly. "You can't possibly set things up without me. I'm the one who knows where we're going, remember?"

"Specifically, yes. For now it's a matter of generalities, and in general, the people I'm going to talk to do not like to deal with strangers. Particularly women."

"I won't be left behind." She put her hands on her hips.

"Look, Minarra, I don't have time to debate this…"

"Really? And given the mess you say things are in, exactly when will it be a good time?"

"When I say so. In the meantime, you are staying here and that's final. And unless you give me your word that you will remain in this room until I come back, I will be forced to take extreme measures."

"Like what?" She snorted.

"Like tying you up."

A dark thrill passed through her belly. A forbidden, needy feeling she dared not voice. They'd come close to bondage in the past. Had they remained together she would eventually have asked for it. "You wouldn't dare."

"Try me," he glowered.

She screwed up her face—ready for another go at him. Then it occurred to her, she could give her word and do what she wanted anyway. After all, wasn't he a liar himself?

"Fine." She sat herself on the bed. "I will stay. Nice as you please."

He lowered his brow. "You're giving in too easily."

"Maybe I'm just tired of fighting," she folded her arms over her breasts.

"That'll be the day," he muttered under his breath. One final check of his suitcase, and he was ready to go. "Don't wait up for me," he told her. "Oh, and by the way," he added at the door. "Just in case you get a hankering to follow me, I am going to ask Osiron to keep a watch over you. Should you attempt to leave the hotel he will notify me immediately."

"Have I ever told you how much I don't like you?" She inquired.

"I've gotten that idea, yes."

"Will you at least tell me where you're going? In case something happens—an emergency?"

He appeared to consider the proposal. "If I do, you won't get ideas about trying to follow? Because I promise you, Osiron has eyes in the back of his head."

Minarra nodded, once again feeling no qualms about making fake promises. "I wouldn't dream of it…"

"It's a place called the Seven Veils. If you need me in an emergency, anyone will know where to find it."

"The Seven Veils?" Minarra stiffened. "What kind of meeting place is that?"

"It's a place where men go. A place you would not be welcomed."

"Why? Is it full of harem girls? Belly dancers? That's it, isn't it?"

"For heaven's sake, Min, what difference does it make? It's not like we're seeing each other or anything."

She flashed an expression of disgust. "As if…"

He rolled his eyes. "Forget I said a word."

"Don't patronize me, Seth Allen Macallister. You think I'm jealous, don't you?"

He put out his hands, the universal sign of male surrender. "I'm not thinking anything—except how to put this expedition together."

"Which is why you need me to go with you. And it shouldn't be at any club full of half-naked hussies either. Anyone who would meet you there isn't the sort we want with us anyway."

"Like I said," he grabbed his safari jacket. "Don't wait up."

Minarra reached for the first thing she could find to throw, which was her left desert boot. It struck the door, a second after his departure.

She clenched her fists. Once again, she'd managed to make a fool of herself, revealing far too much emotion. It was time for calm, time for reason. Opening her attaché case, she took out the map and laid it on the desk. It was approximately eight inches by eight inches and sealed inside a special laminate material, acid free. The clear laminate gave it a glossy, almost modern look.

But there was no mistaking the antiquity of it. The parchment dated to approximately 1200 B.C., which put it in the era of Egypt's Golden Age. Minarra's contention was that it was a copy of something much older, more along the lines of 2600 B.C. Around the edges were scribbled notes and legends, along with encoded sacred symbols. A tiny Ibix-headed human figure, representing Thoth, the Egyptian god of knowledge, a Babylonian lion god, a Safarian two-headed dragon, and many more, all forms of animals and flying creatures.

It was Thoth who pointed with his engraving stick on the map to the place inland from the coast where lay Shera-Sa itself. It was due east of the modern port city of Porto Sayeed, located in what was now nomad territory. Somewhere below the sand, a thousand feet deep. According to the accounts of various Bedouins, backed by legends centuries old, there would sometimes appear

Prisoner of Shera-Sa

lights in the night, glowing beams, of red ruby, blue cobalt and diamond white. Were they some form of beacon? Could there be life somewhere still in Shera-Sa?

The serious scientific community ranked such tales as no more reliable than the legend of Atlantis, whose existence is documented nowhere but in one of Plato's dialogues. Young Roger Hunt had been one of those skeptics until he had occasion himself to encounter the flashing lights, haunting beams, flickers as brilliant as the aurora borealis. It was during a sandstorm. He'd been trapped near a large dune, separated from a party of fellow archeology students. All night, he'd watched for rescuers. That's when he'd had his vision. His eyes would light up each time he recounted it, and to the day he died it remained the single defining moment of his entire life. From that moment on, he had but one thing to live for. And that was finding the city once again. Ironically, in his almost superhuman attempts, he uncovered all his other treasures, several lifetimes' worth.

He also married one of the most beautiful women ever to be born on the island of Corfu and had with her a daughter whom he called his jewel, his vision…his Minarra.

A tear came to Minarra's eye. She placed her palm on the map, which she could not really touch through the plastic. Her father had been that way. So seemingly human, full of bottomless mystery, and inaccessible when it came to his true feelings.

Was it something wrong with her? That men did not wish to be close to her? Mac had run halfway around the world to get away from her…what a fool she felt.

"You're too good for all of them, Minarra," her had father said. "You're like a priceless object…overawing."

Well, she didn't want to be a museum piece. And she didn't want to live only as a curator of them, either. She was a live woman. Witness her dreams. She was so desperate for human contact that she was bringing her research to life, concocting mad princes instead of finding real, healthy men.

Damn Mac for going off so blithely to his Seven Veils. She'd lay odds it was a whorehouse. What gave him the right to play around, leaving her stuck in this room? He could waltz off when he felt like it, leaving her to do all the real work of map reading and then come back and expect her to bow down to his so-called leadership.

It was time to rein this guy in. To teach him a little lesson. He thought he could just turn her passion on and off? Use her when he felt like it? His whore one minute, his academic prop, making him look good the next? Well, he had another think coming. This hotel had a bar, didn't it? She could find herself some trouble right here without breaking out of the prison he'd put her in. That would show him. Yes. She'd go down to the bar, have a couple of drinks, do some flirting. Give Osiron, with those eyes in the back of his head, something to report. She could just picture Mac, getting word and feeling about six inches high for abandoning her. With any luck, she'd make him jealous, too.

She didn't want it to be a petty thing, though. In her mind, it had to be about the expedition—about controlling this man so she could get to Shera-Sa. Her father would approve of it, she was sure.

Yes, by morning he'd be a tamed man, with a whole lot more respect for her capabilities as a woman. It wasn't about making him jealous, either. She hated him, and as far as things went personally, he could drop off the face of the earth. So what if he was out with hookers, letting other women touch him, pleasure him—what did she care? She didn't want him or his body. His fingers, smooth as silk, knowing and skillful, backed by all his manly strength. His eyes, the way they burned and made her feel like the center of the world, like she was the only woman and he was the only man. His nipples, peaking as she kissed them, the way he sighed, approving, needing. The way his hand would move to the back of her head, drawing her in. The way his cock tasted in her mouth when she sucked him, salty-sweet, throbbing and alive, making her feel so totally female and naughty.

The way the muscles in his ass clenched as she touched him there. The way she could come up from behind and rest her cheek against his back, encircling his waist with her arms, her soft curves so completely fitting into his graceful hardness. The way she felt so right being with him...so at home.

Feelings, and sensations, so long buried—all of them unearthed on that airplane, resurrected, making her want and need him all over again...

Oh fuck, this kind of thinking went nowhere.

Opening her suitcase she looked for the most feminine thing she could find, aside from her hopelessly wrinkled outfit from the plane. She was certainly set for khaki...

Minarra sighed. She really did need to work on her wardrobe. Sonya was right about that. Maybe she should call Sonya for advice. Wait—here was something. Her black dress, at the bottom of the case, still in the cleaners' bag. She hadn't remembered packing it. Why had she brought it? Did she expect to be going to a party or dating someone?

It could not have had to do with Mac. That was just not something she'd believe. At any event, it was her key to success tonight. The plan laid itself out in her mind. A quick shower, some makeup and she'd be ready to strut her stuff.

An hour later she was in the lobby, turning heads. Her hair had turned out decently for once—silky and nicely waved down her back. The odds were a million to one, so she took that as a sign the gods were on her side.

The dress fit well, too, thanks to her diet of stress over the past week. She'd even managed to shave her legs without nicking them. A casual observer might have said her relative calm and centered feeling as a woman had to do with her just having had sex with Mac, but she knew better. With her it was all mental, all rational calculation.

Just like Daddy.

Osiron was still at the front desk. His brown eyes got a little wider and his smile broadened. "Miss Hunt," he inclined his head respectfully. "It is a pleasure to see you again this soon. And looking so lovely, too. Had I not three wives already, I would surely propose."

"Thank you, Osiron," she absorbed his warm, safe vibes. "You are a true gentleman. Even if you do need your eyes checked."

He laughed. "Even a blind man would recognize what is beautiful in you. Outside and in."

"I may have to kiss you for that," she teased. "If your wives wouldn't mind."

"What they don't know," he winked. "Won't hurt them."

It was her turn to laugh. "Fair enough. I wonder if you would do me a favor?"

"It would be my honor."

"Mac mentioned you had a way to get hold of him? There's a message I want to leave for him."

Osiron raised an eyebrow. "Yes?"

"Tell him I'll be waiting for him…in the bar."

The other eyebrow went up, though he refrained from any facial expression. "Yes, of course," he offered another of his microscopic bows.

"Thank you, you're a peach."

He cleared his throat. "Miss…if I may take the liberty of saying…"

"Yes?"

"Alcazara is a rather conservative country. Women are not often seen alone, especially in bars."

"Good," she nodded. Better than good — Mac was sure to come running now.

The bar looked like something out of *Casablanca*. Tall potted plants, lazy ceiling fans and rail-thin, sneaky-eyed spy types sipping small, colored drinks. There was a man in a pith helmet and another in a military uniform debating at the bar. A woman in a slinky red dress was gesturing with a long cigarette holder as she spoke to a mutton-chopped man in a black tuxedo. There was a back door through which she saw the flashing lights and colors of the casino.

Two younger Arab men in silk shirts, sleeves rolled up, eyed her as she moved. She was a trifle nervous, but really, how much trouble could she get into? Wouldn't Osiron need to be watching her here, too? Surely he'd protect her. And she'd watch her drinks like a hawk, so no one drugged them.

The bartender wore a white button-down shirt and a red fez. His mustache was long and curled. "A glass of white wine, please," she told him.

The man's lips curled downward. Ignoring her, he proceeded to wipe the top of the bar with a heavy rag.

How rude, she thought. "Excuse me, sir?"

"He will not serve you," came a suave, French accented voice.

She turned to the man. He wore a white linen suit with a crisp red silk tie, matching handkerchief and a perfectly starched pink shirt. His jawline was that of a movie star. He had the eyes, the cheeks, the classic Roman nose, and the wavy black hair. He'd be any woman's wet dream, though oddly she was not attracted.

"Why on earth not?"

"A beautiful woman should never have to stoop to securing her own drinks," he said. "It offends his sensibilities. Will you allow me?"

Minarra considered the man. She preferred Mac's nose, the way it turned down just a little bit, and those eyebrows of his, the way they spoke volumes when he was upset about something. This man just seemed too smooth, too perfect, though he was just the ticket to get Mac's goat.

"Thank you, that would be nice."

The man spoke to the bartender in French. He bowed respectfully and went to fill the order. Eschewing the wine rack at the rear of the bar, he headed to the back room. A short while later he returned with a very old, and obviously very expensive, bottle.

"Maritaigne, sir, '56."

The Frenchman examined the label. "I shall taste it at my usual table in the restaurant," he instructed. "Mademoiselle, would you do me the honor of sharing your company?"

The next thing Minarra knew, she was taking the man's arm, accompanying him to a quiet corner table. Naturally, every head turned to see her with this fabulous man.

"Mademoiselle?" He held out her chair for her.

"To beauty," he toasted, once he'd approved the wine and ordered it poured by the bartender, who'd been standing dutifully by awaiting instructions.

"To beauty," she murmured, producing what she hoped was a dazzling smile. He replied with one of his own, measured and perfectly symmetrical. She could imagine him in front of the mirror, practicing.

She could also imagine the look on Mac's face—very unpracticed—when he saw her with him. If this didn't convince him that she was a woman sought after by men and able to steer her own ship, she thought grimly, nothing would.

Chapter Four

The woman shaking her bare belly mere inches from Mac's face was young and beautiful. Her skin was an unblemished, delicious mocha. As for the rest of her charms, only the tiniest wisps of silk separated his eyes from pure and naked appreciation. Her breasts were full and heavy, the nipples surprisingly pink as they rubbed against the pale blue of her bandeau. She wore pantaloons, also blue. He could make out the fine details of her vaginal mound, covered in trimmed, auburn hair, the same color as her waving tresses. She was barefoot, belled, and also collared.

She was also completely available.

"I think she is in love, my friend," teased Hassan, a bull-necked man with a chest of iron that concealed a heart of gold. "Why not put her out of her misery?"

Two other dancers came in now, a short curvaceous dark-haired girl from the left and a tall, graceful redhead from the right. Each wanted the right to sleep with the American, to be his personal harem girl for the night. Three shapely posteriors bumped at one another as tiny toes dug into the Persian carpeting, a perfect match to the carved ivory fixtures and the decorations of crossed scimitars and round shields on the velvet-draped walls.

It ought to have been a dream come true for any red-blooded American bachelor, but Mac felt nothing for any of them. His sole concern was to conclude the business at hand and get back to Minarra. Leaving her alone had been a bad idea. A woman like that would find trouble to get into. Especially after having her will thwarted so blatantly.

It wasn't that he didn't respect her wisdom or ability. Far from it. It was just that...

He had to pause for a moment. Exactly what was it that caused him not to bring her here? Female guests were allowed, when accompanied by a male. Certainly she knew the language and could hold her own in any negotiations. Could it be, he wondered, that he was simply afraid to let her see the sort of place this was — and to see him, in this element, acting like a typical male predator?

Why would he care what she thought? She already hated him, and he certainly had no personal interest in her.

"She is only being polite to a guest," Mac retorted. "She'd choose you over me any day of the week."

Hassan laughed. Twice he'd had his nose broken and another time he'd butted heads with a camel. It was the camel that had ended up with the concussion. There was no better man to have in your corner. And he wasn't all brawn, either. His father had been the advisor to a desert chieftain. He knew more about the myths and legends of Shera-Sa than anyone, with the exception of Minarra herself. "Don't waste your flattery on me — save it for your female conquests."

The other three men at the table — bearded, robed camel drivers with bandoliers of bullets strung across their shoulders — slapped the table good-naturedly in agreement. The four of them would form the core of the expedition's transportation and security force. Hassan would hire any additional men and would also arrange for camels to be delivered to them in the desert once they had run out of roads to drive on.

"I know better than to argue with you, Hassan," Mac retorted, feeling in less than top condition to trade barbs with his friend. "All the more reason to seal the deal quickly."

"My friend," Hassan shook his head sadly. "Don't tell me you have finally given in to the work ethic? We were put in this world to play—and what better thing to play with than a woman?" He snapped his fingers, signaling to the curvy little delight to come and sit on his lap. She did so eagerly.

For a split second, Mac thought of having Minarra sitting on his lap, scantily clad in red silk, her lips parted and eager, her eyes moist, and her body hot with anticipation. His hand, drifting to her thigh, a little moan escaping her throat as he told her what awaited her that night, in his tent under the stars...

* * * * *

"Yes," she sighed, arching her neck, inviting his touch further up. His hand slid up her belly to her bandeau, to her barely covered breasts.

"You will dance for me, my slave...you will show me your charms, that body of yours which is mine to own, mine to possess...mine to control."

"Yes...Master."

He threw her to her back on the table and ripped away her clothes. "Open for me," he commanded, compelling her to spread her legs for penetration.

His cock, hard as steel, a glinting sword, would pierce her wetness to the hilt. Her lips singing surrender, her bare, bangled ankles, would lock behind him. Arms tossed overhead, laid out in capitulation, back arched, soft, exquisite, delicate breasts heaving, she begged to be manipulated, kissed, suckled...bitten.

He caught her wrists in his hands, and she looked into his eyes, begging in wonder for him to take her all the way, to never stop, and yet so very terrified of where he would take her. Belly to belly, the spasms built, just as they had in the restroom of the airplane, all the old fires igniting, the old combustion hotter than ever. Their ability to please each other, to come in soul-shattering bliss...

* * * * *

"Sir," the waiter was bowing, right beside Mac's ear.

He snapped himself back into reality. Damn—he'd nearly come in his pants daydreaming about Minarra. While sitting in a roomful of eager belly dancers, no less. "Yes, what is it?"

"There is a message for you, from your hotel."

His radar went up immediately. "Minarra..." he said aloud.

"Excuse me, sir?"

"Nothing, it's nothing. What is the message?"

"It is from the manager. He says simply, "Scorpion eying blue-eyed prize—Contained."

Fuck.

"I am sorry, sir, if this makes no sense?"

"No, I understand fine," he said grimly. "Gentlemen, I apologize." He was on his feet. "I have something I must attend to."

"But the negotiations," one of the bearded men protested.

"I'll agree to whatever number Hassan thinks is fair…divided by two. Bring me the contract to sign in the morning."

He left them laughing, all four pounding the table in great enthusiasm. "Now that, my friends," he heard Hassan say, "is a man after my own heart."

Mac hired the fastest-looking taxi outside the club and handed the man triple the usual fare to step on it back to the hotel. Osiron was still at the desk—a post he occupied an average of sixteen hours a day. Angling his eyebrows up and slightly right he indicated that Minarra was still in the bar.

With *him*.

He did a double take, seeing her in the sexy black dress. It was a far cry from the usual khaki. Under different circumstances he'd have stood in quiet awe. As it was, he was going to have to extricate her from a black hole.

"Monsieur Macallister," greeted the white-suited man, known to police on three continents as Scorpion. "What a pleasant surprise. Won't you join us for a glass of wine? You've no objection, do you, Minarra? This man is an old friend."

"I'm not a friend of yours," Mac challenged. "And I won't be staying. Nor will she."

"Don't speak for me, Mac Macallister. I'm perfectly capable of deciding with whom I spend my time."

"Evidently not," he snarled. "Now are you coming quietly or must I drag you out?"

"Go to hell!" She defied.

"Am I to assume," said Scorpion, "that you two are acquainted?"

"Yes, we are," said Minarra. "Though at times like this I wish we weren't."

"Is that right, Minarra? How about if I give you a proper introduction to your new friend? Or, did you already tell her about yourself, Henri?"

Henri pursed his lips, curling them into a sadistic smile. "I may have left out a salient detail or two."

"In that case, allow me to introduce Henri Louis Foucault, better known as Scorpion. Wanted in four countries for kidnapping, extortion, trafficking in human beings."

"It's five countries, actually," he corrected. "And I prefer to think of myself as a global entertainment director."

"Henri is a slave trader, Minarra. He steals women and sells them, for use as sex slaves and brothel prostitutes."

Minarra's mouth hung open a bit. She looked back and forth between the two men.

"Let's go, Min," he took her hand. "Now."

He was furious by the time they reached the suite. She must have sensed something, too, because she wasn't offering any of her usual rationalizations and defenses.

"I'm tired," she announced as he closed the door behind them. "I'm going to bed. I'll ask you to have the courtesy to sleep out here on the couch."

That was it. The proverbial straw to put the camel in traction. "You want *me* to have courtesy? *You're* tired?"

"That's what I said, Mac, yes. And if you're going to start repeating everything I say, I can tell you up front it's going to wear a little thin."

"I'm so sorry," he dripped sarcasm. "If I'm cramping your style. Has it occurred to you, young lady, the potential hazards you put yourself in by disobeying my orders tonight?"

She put her hands on her hips. *Damn it, why did she have to be so totally, completely irresistible?*

"First of all," she informed him. "You're not giving me any orders. Second of all, you only told me not to leave the hotel, you never said anything about the bar."

Mac frowned. She was right. "All right, so I didn't spell it out—but you had no business being with that man, Min. As good as he looks on the outside, he's total scum. I can understand the sexual attraction as a woman, but you'd have wound up chained somewhere to a bed turning tricks twenty hours a day. Women are nothing but commodities to him, Min."

"Actually, for your information, I wasn't attracted to him at all, but thanks for selling me so short. As for him just wanting to use me, seems like that's the pot calling the kettle black. Especially after what happened on the airplane."

"How was I using you? You said yourself what happened between us on the airplane was you, using me."

"It doesn't matter. I'm talking about your intentions. You came in that bathroom to fuck me, Mac. You figured that I was vulnerable and you were horny…same old story, right? You snap your fingers, I roll over for you…"

She laughed, no trace of humor evident in her voice. "What a sucker I am. I can't even believe how I fooled myself, acting like it could be different. It's never different. You take what you want, and I give. Poor, simple Minarra—doesn't know the world, doesn't know what's good for her. Too bad you ran off, babe. Daddy would have married me off to you in a heartbeat so you could take his place."

"Min, I'm going to explain all this one day, and you are going to—"

She had her hands over her ears. She was trying to walk right past him. "Forget it, Mac. I won't listen anymore."

He had her arm in a vise grip. Where do you think you're going?"

She was trying to pull away, her eyes spoiling for a fight. "I'm leaving the fucking room...asshole. Now let go of me."

He held her firmly. "You're acting like a spoiled brat."

"Screw you." She was squirming for all she was worth.

"Settle down, Min." His tone was firm, no-nonsense, though it elicited a stream of curses in response.

Enough was enough.

Mac lifted her into his arms and carried her to the bed. Minarra continued to wriggle and kick at him until he deposited her on her belly on the mattress. He'd administered a few erotic spankings in his day, but this would be the first time he'd be disciplining an unruly female for her own good.

"Get the fuck off me! I'll scream rape!'

He pressed a single palm to the small of her back, holding her down. "If you insist on screaming, I will gag you. Now calm down, no one's being raped. You're going to be spanked, that's all."

"Spanked!? You can't be serious. That's...that's immoral."

"I'm deadly serious. As commander of this expedition, I will keep discipline by whatever means required, including corporal punishment.

"You're insane, Seth Macallister!"

He swatted her, none too lightly. "You'll thank me for this later."

"Ow! That hurt you bastard!"

He felt a tiny bit guilty for the phenomenal hard-on he was acquiring in the midst of her ordeal. The way her perfect, heart-shaped ass was wriggling, the way she felt — under his power, at his mercy. "The only thing being injured is your pride," he declared.

"I hate you," she spat. "I'll always hate you and I'll never forgive you."

"I think you need to take this bare-assed," he decided. "Let's get these clothes off you."

"You're a pig," she wailed. "A brute and an animal."

He unzipped the back of the dress, running his hand down the small of her back. Her skin was so smooth and warm and alive. It was taking all his willpower not to have at her right there. He could take his cock, put it right between those ass cheeks...

"Lift your hips," he ordered, enforcing the decree with a fresh spank.

She cried out, doing as she'd been told. He took the opportunity to work the dress up to her waist, fully exposing her panties. "Turn over, put your hands over your head."

"Mac, this is crazy..." She was less defiant now, more plaintive. There was a note of desperation, too, though they both knew damned well it had nothing to do with her being forced or abused. If she had anything to fear here, it was not Mac but rather her own desires. Their sexuality had always been deep and complicated. One dimension of it involved dominance and submission...it was a rich vein, fraught with emotion, one they had barely begun to explore.

"It may be crazy," he informed her. "But it's going to continue."

Indeed, he had every intention of introducing her to bondage in short order. He told himself this had no meaning right now except for the expedition, for discipline, to teach her a lesson that might save her life later on, but maybe he was kidding himself. Maybe it was all about the sex. All about his own desperation to win Minarra back."

"Look, Mac, you win. I concede...whatever you want me to say or do."

He pulled the dress over her head. "It's not that simple, Min. This is punishment. There's no getting out of it."

"No, it's not. It's sadism. Otherwise you wouldn't need me naked to gawk over me, and you most certainly wouldn't have that erection."

"Stop being melodramatic," he chided. "And for your information, I've never been turned on by pain, only by sexual domination, free and consensual."

"So you admit it! You want me to agree to play some sicko sex game."

Min was managing to break through his precariously arranged logic. "It's not sick, it's not a game, and it's not… Oh Christ, Min, don't act like we haven't been here before. You were never wetter than when I came up from behind and 'forced' myself on you, or when I held your hands down and had my way with you."

Mac tossed the dress onto the floor and was promptly rewarded with a crisp smack across the cheek. "There's some power play right back at you. How do you like it?"

Minarra had never looked more exciting to him, her hair wild, stripped to her underwear, a delicious, cornered little wildcat. He could pounce on her right now, and in seconds they'd be writhing, willing and eager, a tangle of sweaty, consensual limbs.

On the other hand, he could take them somewhere else—by taking her over, seizing control of her desires in a different way. There was, after all, a precedent between them…a particular incident.

"You're going to do what I say, Min." His voice was calm, supremely gentle, but unyielding. "You're going to obey. You'll start by taking off your bra and panties for me."

Her sweet, glossy pink little toes dug into the gold, brocaded bedspread, a rich enhancement to the four rounded posts of dark mahogany. "Mac this has gone far enough…"

He noted the quickness of her breathing, the way she was unconsciously holding in her concave stomach and pushing out her breasts as she lay back on her palms. There was no disguising it, the look in her eyes, the slight gap between her thighs. Mac knew this woman as well as he knew himself, maybe better. She wanted it as much as he.

Was she thinking of the same occasion?

"Remember the night in the dunes, Minarra?"

Her eyes flashed with torturous heat, the memory burning through her body with the fresh, searing heat of the desert sun, a golden arrow, dissolving her soul. That particular night was the closest they had come to inhabiting the dark side of sex. One did not forget such things...ever.

"That was six years ago, Mac." She was fighting to keep her voice steady. Rational. "Ancient history. Deader than the pharaohs."

Mac put his hand to the side of her neck, the other on her belly. "Is it?" he called her bluff, his teeth nibbling her ear with agonizing softness.

Her nerve endings opened like floodgates, the blood rushing to the surface of her skin, a million tiny orgasms erupted in the cells of her body as she anticipated his next move.

He'd always been able to do this—calm and focus her, while at the same time driving her wild with desire. In turn, she had given him a reason to be a man.

"Kiss me," he said, his mouth an inch from hers.

Minarra's lips fell open. But she could no longer have kept from craning her neck, then puckering her lips, than she could have from breathing.

The kiss was a hot, searing brand, a slithering conquest of her tongue, a lowering to a place of wicked subjugation. And as much as she might not want to go there, part of her did…and he was taking her.

"Start with the bra," he coached, allowing her to breathe.

She moved as in a trance, reaching behind her back.

"Do it slowly."

Minarra unhooked the clasp and slid the shoulder straps forward, one at a time, as she shed the cups, revealing her full, glorious globes, as yet impervious to gravity.

"You're so incredibly beautiful," he declared fiercely, intent on sending a fresh fiery arrow through her heart. "You eclipse even your mother, you know that?"

She flushed delicately at the praise, but dared not refuse it under the current circumstances.

"Play with your nipples, Min. Make them hard."

He watched her features shift, like glistening sand. Behind her eyes, she was drifting back to the dunes…

* * * * *

…a single night, trapped in a sandstorm, not unlike what had happened to Minarra's father. Except they had not been graced by visions from the desert, no fleeting ghost lights from Shera-Sa to point out their destiny. What they came to understand instead was the true power of passion between two individuals. It had been absolutely naked and primal and desperately glorious. The searing rush of sand over their heads, the roar of the black darkness obscuring the stars and the noses in front of their faces. The world that threatened to swallow them whole, like dry quicksand.

Their mating was a form of ultimate exhibitionism — performing before the might of the desert, the crackling dry, heaving lightning of the gods, the rain that teased but never quite materialized, the unseen vista that threatened to open to space itself.

Minarra was face down, half on and off their emergency blanket, clutching at the sand, her breasts and belly pressed into the dune, her body shielded and swallowed whole by his. Equally naked, shielding her with utter animalistic power — protection and fierce lust rolled into one — he took her from behind.

They shut out the world and took it in all at once. She was so tight, such a supremely perfect fit. Over and over she moaned to be taken, fucked and used, had and made whole.

"Min," he cried, his voice barely carrying over the storm. "I love you."

She cried out as he came, filling her with his pent-up fluids. His erection felt as though it had swollen to twice its normal size. He was clutching at her, teeth sinking into her shoulder, hands grabbing greedily at her slender waist, just above the curve of her perfect, woman's hips. Her body was writhing in the sand with his, reaching up, connecting and sharing, though she had not yet reached her own climax.

Mac's erection barely diminished as he rolled her over, on top of him. Placing her on his cock, he slipped deep inside. Her groans were pure female, pure pre-orgasmic surrender.

Falling forward, she dug her nails into his chest. "Oh god," she moaned. "I need to come."

It was then that he felt the full measure of that love he had just proclaimed. The words, the soft sentiment was not enough. He needed more...she needed more.

"Not until I say." Mac grabbed her sand-blasted hair, a wild corona with all the fury of a witch's cape. Bowing her back, exposing her torso fully to his whims, he placed his free hand on her breast. Kneading it.

Minarra whimpered, teeth gritted. It was deliberate, almost cruel. But he was determined to brand her mind, to associate with him a pleasure she would never feel anywhere else. It was totally a matter of trust on her part, and indeed she gave herself fully.

Mac denied her, time and again bringing her to the brink, and then pulling her back. It was a stark lesson that a woman on top need not be in control at all. At last the storm began to clear, the stars returned, and Mac gave her the opportunity.

"Beg for it, Min."

"Mac, please..." Her eyes were those of a different woman, her lips spoke from a deeper place. She'd gone to another level, one they would lose all too soon, but which, in that moment, ruled their spiritual destiny. "May I...let me..."

He spoke the word "Yes"...

* * * * *

From that night, to this moment, it was there, unspoken but real. Sometimes alluded to in subsequent lovemaking, but never invoked. Until now.

Here in this hotel room, given a second chance with this woman he'd never expected to see again, let alone share intimacy with. Filled with heat and wonder and passion, he took in the sight of her, pleasuring herself, touching her nipples under his command…almost as if she was his.

* * * * *

Minarra cursed her weakness, her inability to say no. *Damn it*, she thought, nipples hardening obediently between her thumbs and forefingers, *why am I doing this? Why am I letting myself go back to that other place, that other time? I'm not the same woman, not the same naïve coed, completely overwhelmed by the brawn and intellect and will of this one man… So incredibly beautiful to look at, so dangerous to touch.*

She sought to rally her resolve before it was too late. She had to focus on the immediate reality. The reality of Mac Macallister. The real scorpion in her life.

"Are you wet for me?" He wanted to know, seeking to breach her deepest intimacies.

She sucked her lower lip, fighting to hold onto her pride. "Nothing in me is for you, Mac…it hasn't been in forever."

"So? Is it so wrong to want to go back? Just this once? Don't deny me," he said huskily, his hand resting on her thigh. "Don't deny us."

"You have no right…"

His lips softened. "Please?"

Never had Minarra heard this man beg. He'd made her beg, on the dunes that night. He'd shown her that part of herself that craved to be owned by a male. Now he was showing her something else. Giving her a chance to show mercy and strength herself.

Minarra lowered her eyes. How could she resist now? Having come this far? Sliding her hand over her belly, past his, shivering at her own heat, she reached the waistband of her panties.

He was waiting patiently. "Tell me, Min."

"Yes," she whispered, the lips of her sex thrumming against her fingertips. Her eyes slid closed, it was like a waking dream, his voice holding the power of a hypnotist. "I'm wet."

"You were always ready for me," he confirmed. "I never met a woman so completely sexual as you. You get wet with just a look."

Only from you, she thought, though she would never, ever let him know that.

"You want to please me, don't you, Min? You want to give yourself…to let me do as I will."

His affirmation of power over her, spoken almost in a whisper, sent a fresh rush to her loins. At the same time, she felt a surge of rebellion. "But who's really in charge, Mac? If these are my fantasies…isn't it you, serving me?"

He gave her a wink, his luscious lips curling into a cool, delectable smile. Mac was playing the bad boy now. "Take off your panties, Min, before I rip them. Then I want you on all fours, showing me your naked ass."

Her breathing was short and tight, sweet little stabs, each intake sending little ripples through her chest and crotch. There was no denying him now. She lifted her ass, tugging down the sopping wet underwear. Ankle by ankle, she removed it. Mac gazed down on her hungrily, making her feel like the beautiful creature he said she was. She managed to make a little show, flexing each calf, stretching her toes. Mac made her feel safe this way, free to surrender and be a woman…naked under a man's control.

A man who was obviously as desirous of her as she was of him.

"Wait…take the covers down."

She helped him expose the sheets, Egyptian cotton, onyx black, with an irresistibly high thread count. Just feeling the material on her palms was almost enough to make her come on the spot.

Minarra got on her hands and knees, facing the headboard. Her pulse quickened in dread anticipation. She could no longer see what he was doing. For a few seconds, she felt and heard nothing from him. Her ears strained. She licked sweat from her lips. Was it her or was the room growing damper?

The fan was oscillating overhead. Outside she heard the short, staccato bleep of a siren, so different than the ones at home. God, her pussy was pulsing, waiting to suck anything in that came near. Her buttocks felt every little vibration in the air.

She tried to blow the stray hairs that had plastered themselves to her cheeks. Her every muscle ached with energy. She was not sure if she would faint first or explode.

Suddenly, she felt his fingertips. Minarra jolted in reaction. She did her best not to squirm away or get up and run. Gripping the silk with her nails, she submitted to his touch.

"I'm going to spank you," he rubbed her behind, calming her shivering body. "And then I'm going to take you in the ass."

Minarra moaned at his caress, so very light and yet so completely...possessive. The way he was talking...like she really belonged to him after all these years. Not only that, he was intending to go further than they ever had before. "But Mac, I'm...I'm a virgin back there."

"There's a first time for everything."

"Oh god..." He was playing with her clit, manipulating it with a single fingertip, distracting her. "Must you cheat at every turn?"

Mac laughed. His hand collided with her ass, the spank coming out of nowhere. "As much as I can. Tell me something," he changed the subject. "What did you intend to do in that dress?"

She shook her head, as he delivered another blow, hot liquid sensation, tingling fire across her posterior. "Nothing," she yelped. "I just put it on."

"Don't lie to me." He made her pay with another swat. It was so much worse this way, with no clothes to protect her. And yet at the same time, it was driving her wild. "You hate dressing up. You'd sooner spend a night alone in Mahopet's Tomb covered in beetles than wear a dress."

"You don't know me like you think," she defied.

"Is that right?" He snorted. "Well let's try this on for size. You were trying to make me jealous, playing the *femme fatale* with that scum Henri because I was going to the Seven Veils."

Minarra winced against the double bull's-eye — one from a fresh spank, the other from his assessment of her behavior. Much as she hated to admit it, there really was no other logical reason for her going down to the bar much less sitting with Scorpion.

But why make a man jealous when you don't even want him?

"You're an arrogant prick if you think that," she insisted. "Anyway," she multiplied her smokescreen. "I couldn't be a *femme fatale* to save my life."

He went to work on her clitoris. "You think I'm blind to your charms? You're the most gorgeous fucking woman in this country—in any country. You can have any man you want. I've known that from the day I met you. You're one in a million, probably a billion."

Her heart raced to hear his words. Could it be true? Could he really see her that way? "Your loss for dumping me, then, huh?"

Mac flicked his finger, bringing her to whimpering, shattering surrender. Once again, he was conveniently sidestepping the primary issue of their past.

"I care about now. You're under my command. For the rest of this expedition, you'll obey me. Without hesitation, because your life depends on it, I promise."

He went to work, alternating his caresses with artful spanks. He was systematic, yet thoroughly devious in his approach. Pain and pleasure blended, the trickling sex fluids running down her fire-ridden thighs. She was crying, begging for release, not even sure what she wanted. She found herself craving spanks, and begging for the touches to stop. Her senses were a mess. Twice she fell onto her belly and was ordered back to her hands and knees for further punishment.

At a certain point, as abruptly as it had started, the ordeal stopped. She felt the displacement as he rose from the bed, leaving her, her ass throbbing. She was sure it was beet-red—red and puffy like her sex lips, oozing the liquid of her feminine subjugation. To her humiliation, her hips kept moving, grinding the air, and seeking his touch, his slaps, and his pinches—anything except to be left in total ignorance and helplessness like this.

Where had he gone? Why had he ceased his torture?

The lights clicked out. Minarra stiffened, on the verge of an abyss. It was the dunes all over again, except the storm was in her heart, in her mind.

"Mac?" She whispered, scarcely daring to break the silence. A sheen of sweat turned cold on her body, and still she burned. Somewhere in the distance, she could smell the scent of him, musk and testosterone. And incense, burning somewhere outside the window. A slow, smoldering odor, the combined sins of a thousand bodies, a thousand, aching yearning years.

"Hush," he called back. His voice instantly calmed her frayed, lightning-edged nerves.

His hand was at her cheek. She rubbed against it, needing the contact of his skin. Her nipples ached as if they were ready to explode. She wanted him inside her so much…

"It's time," he told her.

She took a breath, savoring her own exquisite uncertainty. "Mac, I…"

"No more words," he cut her off.

It had been a close call. Had he known she was about to profess love? It would have been the first time, too. Why had that not occurred to her before, she wondered? Mac had told her he loved her that night in the dunes, but she had never said the words back. Not then, or ever. She was too much like her father. He held his cards to his vest, preferring to live through other passions, most especially his work and after that his obsession to control the natural environment, his family first and foremost.

"I want you to concentrate on being open, Min. And ready."

She gasped at the feel of the cool ointment. He rubbed it across her backside, soothing the raging fires. The residue of the spanking cooled to a dull ache, a pleasant glow that made her want to slip down to her belly...

There was little time to rest, however, as his fingers quickly moved into her anus, lubricating the tight, virgin canal.

"You don't know, Min, how long I dreamed of this." His voice was husky, so seemingly heartfelt. One could almost forget his true colors, his actions that spoke so much louder than his words of love.

Had he missed her, she wondered, even a moment these last six years—even to the extent of imagining an act of perverted sex with her? If so, there was no way she would ever have known, since he'd made no attempt whatsoever to contact her in all this time. Apparently it would have been too much for the great Mummy Hunter to face the pain he'd caused. All the nights she'd cried hot tears—the times she'd put her hand between her legs in desperation and rage, trying to come close to duplicating what they'd had—the times she'd cursed his name, even as she'd pleaded to the invisible gods to return him to her.

She'd been forced to live in self-imposed exile, totally divorced from her own feelings. Dating had been impossible. Even wearing a swimsuit was problematic because of an odd neurosis she'd developed. A fear that somehow, some semblance of the brand that he'd threatened in jest to place on her upper thigh, would show.

Mac's hands on her waist were strong as steel now, enveloping, possessing. But they were protecting, too. She could not imagine a better pair of male hands on this entire planet. Where else could she feel so much herself — so completely...in place?

Wanted. Had. Cherished.

"Oh god," he sighed, his cock piercing the twin globes. "Oh sweet god."

Min moaned, willing herself open, craving his penetration. It was happening...the letting go he'd spoken of. He would never be able to hold her to this. It would have no meaning beyond the moment, but still, it was there — the tenderness in the darkness. "Go deep," she urged, all thoughts of their enmity gone for the moment. "Go as deep as you want."

Her words seemed to galvanize him. His initial thrust was completely masterful, measured, smooth and uncompromising. Minarra cried out — impaled.

It was like the dunes all over again, under the wild star winds, the rushing air of thunder and flash of lightning, with its teasing promise of rain.

Only now they were older. They'd suffered, each in their own desert. Dare she hope for something...anything out of this new coupling?

Mac was groaning like a man possessed. She had him past the point of rational control. He was a man fucking his woman — fucking *her* — and right now, there was no other woman for him on the whole fucking earth and if one even came near him, Min would scratch out her eyes.

"I'm gonna..." Mac could hardly get the words out.

Minarra cheered him on. "Yes. Come in my ass, Mac... I'm here, Mac... I'm here...for you to use..."

She relished the fullness, the pressure. Her aching, open pussy drew pleasure vicariously. She became her own call—the voice of yearning and urging—the wanting, the seduction itself.

There was something familiar in it, something that pulsed through her swaying breasts, radiating from out of her bullet-like nipples. It was coming from the tips of her fingers and toes and reverberating through her flat belly. Sensations from every part of her body, colliding in her mind, tripping the trigger of something that was at once fantasy, memory and vision.

I'm here...for you to use...

That voice...could it belong to the other Minarra? Calling out afresh to her prince. To the Komen-tah of her dreams? Could it be there was more in all this than dust from a long forgotten past, more than a legend...more even than her dreams?

* * * * *

Mac withdrew at the last second, opting to spurt his come over Minarra's pinkened backside. At the same time, he hooked a finger inside her, stimulating her to an instant and powerful orgasm. She made such an incredible target, such a dazzling sight, his shooting spurts of come landing on her, dabbing across the surface of her rocking, shaking body. He milked his cock furiously, his hand rubbing up and down the thick, purple-hued shaft, squeezing out every last drop.

The sounds of her pleasure filled his ears, giving him as much joy as the climax itself. He could smell her sweet release—how well he recalled the taste of those precious fluids. There was her perfume, too, and the electric sound of her breath, the vital feel of her skin, the way she looked and sighed, the silk of her hair, the arch of her back. It was the total package, all the sensations, and the mutuality between them. Perfect, just as it had always been with Minarra.

"So fucking...incredible..." he voiced, straining to put the words together.

Minarra collapsed with a final, soft mewl of pleasure, ending up on her belly, arms stretched overhead. The emotions that rose in him, seeing her like this, were almost too much to bear. Already fresh desire was stirring, and yet at the same time, he wanted to cover her and protect her. What this poor woman had been through. Losing him, and then a year later her father. The fact that he had not been able go to her and comfort her was the greatest pain and shame he would ever know in his life.

Compared to that, the machete wound in South America, the bullet he'd had lodged in his rib cage in Ulterra, and even the time he'd been at death's door with Crane's Fever had been like mere scratches.

If only she would let him in now...if only he were man enough to try. Seeing her like this, so vulnerable and spent in the wake of passion, so seemingly open to him, he could almost believe it was so, that they could still be one. Mac locked his jaws. Damn it, he was on the verge of tears. He had to get to the bathroom fast.

To his surprise she grabbed vaguely at his arm. "Don't go," she slurred, her cheek pressed to the mattress, her hair covering her face in a delightful and sexy corona.

He laid a hand on the small of her back. "I'll just be gone a minute," he offered softly.

"Promise?"

"Scout's honor." He bent to kiss her neck. She sighed in warm anticipation, lifting her neck ever so slightly. So she was still ready to live in this moment, this suspension of time between a tragic past and an empty future. It was more than he could have hoped for. Already he could feel his cock hardening again. This time it would be slow and leisurely, and in the end, she would take his semen deep inside herself, down her canal—that sweet, hot channel he'd once known like a part of his own body, and whose contours he'd imagined every time he'd been with another woman since.

Oh god, he wanted to do everything to her, kiss and talk to her, fuck her and tie her...whatever it took to make sure she never left again. But he couldn't go back to that place, mentally. He couldn't put her through that kind of emotional exhuming. There were things better left dead and buried.

Roger had told him once, when first they began to work together, when it had become clear that he would be his protégé, that there was an inevitable curse associated with any process of archeology. *To dig up the artifacts, the bones—it is all a form of desecration. And yet because our own psyches are so tormented by the past, we are driven to do so anyway, no matter what sentence the gods decree.*

"Don't let me sleep," she mumbled, lost in some world of twilight consciousness. "Love me."

Mac smiled through tears at her plea. If only she knew how much he'd suffered without her. The color had been ripped from his world, half his own heart, torn from his chest. Had he been a coward to not fight for her? To allow Roger Hunt's will and opinions to override his own? Irony of ironies — the old man had driven Mac away to spare her from a life as an archeologist's widow, and yet she'd become one herself.

"Be right back," he reiterated with a whisper in her ear. "Wait here."

She reached for him again. "I mean it, Mac. Don't let me sleep."

The remark puzzled him for its vehemence, but he simply nodded, assuring her. Gently extricating himself from the bed now, leaving her body, beautifully reposed, he went to the bathroom. The tile was cool under his feet, though the room itself was warm. It was always warm in Alcazara. One had the choice here of warm, hot and scorching, depending on time of year and location.

The fixtures in the bathroom were antique bronze and brass, from the early part of the last century. Counts had stayed in this suite, and earls and perhaps a prime minister or two. They'd had their consorts, their courtesans, but none had ever held a woman like Minarra in their arms. She was more than any man deserved, him included.

Looking at his reflection in the round, gilded mirror set on the light yellow wall, he saw his age showing in tiny ways under his eyes, in the slight lines at the edges of his mouth. There seemed to be a little less glint in his eyes, too. He was getting tired. Tired of running around the globe. Running from his past. And yet there was no way back.

Mac put a washcloth under the faucet, soaking it. Pure, cleansing water. He was about to tend to his cock when he felt the familiar press of a body behind him, hot, eager.

So much for waiting for him.

"Your obedience is lacking," he teased. "As usual."

"Shut up," Minarra turned him around and took the cloth from his hands. "And deal with it."

Minarra proceeded to wipe him clean, her small fingers lavishing exquisite attention over every inch of his cock and balls. He breathed an impassioned sigh. After a few initial wipes, she wrapped the cloth about his cock, forming a tube.

"Min," he whispered his appreciation as she applied light pressure, just the way she knew he loved.

Minarra shook her hair over her left shoulder and moved in to kiss his chest. One by one, she nibbled at his nipples. The nubs swelled in her mouth. He laid his hand on the back of her neck, enjoying the silkiness of her hair.

"Mmm…" he offered gratefully, opting not to ruin the moment with words.

No other woman's lips had ever held this magic for him. The way she pressed and challenged and invited. Indeed, it was everything about her. Her scent, like roses, fresh day and night, the sounds of her breathing, so deeply expressive.

He watched as she turned the faucet on, tossing in the cloth. She was after the soap now, tearing it from the wrapper. It had some fancy label. Mac never cared about things like that, but Min did. He found it an endearing part of her how she'd squirreled away in her desert gear a few feminine touches, tiny bottles of perfume and a small vial of lotion.

The combination of her extraordinary femininity and beauty with her tomboyish attitude and brilliant mind had made her irresistible from the moment he'd laid eyes on her.

Min lathered up her hands, covering them with thick white suds. She had a wicked look in her eyes and it didn't take a rocket scientist to guess what she intended to do next.

He released a low groan, distinctly male, as she replaced the cloth with the slick, creamy lather. It was rich and smooth and cool. He hardened completely almost at once, delighting in the feel of himself throbbing in her palms. Deciding turnabout was fair play, he grabbed the wet soap and began to apply the lather to her as well. Before they knew it they were both laughing like old times, their bodies flush and ripe with the pleasure of each other's devotions.

"We need more water," Mac decided, leading her to the shower.

Minarra stood with him in the round marble stall as the miniature downpour erupted over their heads. He adjusted the creaking knobs, fixing the temperature. Min was busy with the soap, wanting it seemed, to cover every inch of him.

No man had ever been that *dirty to require so much cleaning*, he thought with a wry grin. Of course it was an excuse. Her palms slid over his skin, she squeezed his ass cheeks, and pressed her slick breasts against him as the water sluiced between their bodies. His shaft was rigid, poking between her thighs. He moaned at the feel of her, nipple to nipple, her small feet planted atop his to give her added height. His hands slid down to cup her ass cheeks. He his teeth nibbled the flesh of her neck as water rolled down over his eyes and the bridge of his nose.

Mac was all set to lift her up onto him, to impale her against the wall, but Minarra had a different idea. Shaking him off, she dug her nails into his chest. Raking downward. Down to the floor of the stall. Down to her knees. She bit at him, playfully, up and down the length of his cock, her hands weighing his full, heavy balls.

For a virgin, Min had proved herself phenomenal at fellatio. She'd credited it at the time to his ability to put her at ease, to make her feel so sexy and willing to take chances. She'd certainly taken chances the very first time, leaning across to him at the morning camp briefing, whispering in his ear that afterwards, she was going to take him to the digs for something different. They'd only been having sex for a week at that point.

"I'm gonna give you the blowjob of your life," she'd said, her father sitting less than ten feet away at the head of the table. "I want you to come in my mouth, so I can swallow every drop."

"Young man, what on earth are you on about?" Roger had demanded, seeing the look on Mac's face.

Minarra had sat next to him, thoroughly enjoying his predicament.

"It's nothing, sir." Mac cleared his throat. "Nothing at all."

The old man shook his head. "This is what we are dealing with," he addressed the other two senior professors, "in our younger generation."

Minarra had earned a good tickling later for being such a little imp, but she'd been true to her word. At the bottom of a twenty-foot hole, out of sight of the rest of the expedition, she'd sucked his cock deep to the back of her throat, making him come after just a few motions of her beautiful head. To the last drop, just as she'd said, she swallowed his come.

This time it was water surrounding them. Running his hands through her sopping wet hair, he gloried in her. She was like a sea nymph, a water sprite, with the body of a lush goddess and the mind of a genius. And here she was, devoting herself completely, to him.

He let himself go to the back of her throat. She pressed her teeth along the underside, pressuring the thick vein. It was one of those instinctive things she knew how to do. Feeling himself swell, tangling his fingers in her hair, he anticipated coming this way.

But he wouldn't do that, not tonight. He had more exploring to do, more expressing, playing and catching up. Turning off the water behind him, Mac helped Minarra to her feet.

She looked at him questioningly, at which point he swept her up into his arms. "Back to bed," he winked.

She was laughing by the time he rolled her onto the mattress. He followed her, pinning her down, wrists overhead. "Your favorite position," he murmured. "Remember?"

The look on her face spelled pure mischief. She didn't exactly knee him in the groin, but she did manage to press home the point. "Actually," she smiled, sweet as pie. "I was rather fond of this one, too."

He arched a brow. Apparently she was no longer in a submissive mindset. "Didn't anyone ever tell you not to point a loaded weapon?"

Minarra pushed harder against his balls. "Daddy always told me, you need your own weapons to fight your own battles."

An ironic statement, Mac noted, coming from a man who'd tried to fight all of Minarra's battles for her, including trying to control her choice of whom to love.

"But you have to remember," he pointed out. "Your opponents have weapons, too." He stuck out his tongue, giving her a clue as to just what instrument he intended to use on her and how.

Minarra squealed as he made his attack, grabbing her ankle and swinging it wide. A heartbeat later he had her helpless, legs scissored in the air. "Now there," he admired her exposed pussy, the pink lips puffy and slightly parted in unwitting invitation, "is a view."

Min wriggled and bucked in mock distress. "Bully."

"Tell me you hate it."

"I hate it."

He grinned. "Liar."

She folded her arms over her breasts. "Whatever," she stuck up her nose. "Just go on...ravish me and get it over with."

"And let you off the hook so easily? I don't think so. I intend to make this last a good long time."

"Uh-huh." This time she put her hand over her mouth, feigning a yawn. "In that case, wake me when you're through."

"Witch," he laughed. "I'll show you."

She cried out, fighting back laughter as he dove between her thighs, mouthfirst. Mac had always loved going down on Minarra, especially when she was feeling feisty. Nothing like a little taming by his tongue to get her in line quickly — like a tiny whip back and forth over her clit. Min thrashed, lifting her hips.

"Bastard," she growled, good-naturedly.

"Want me to stop?"

"Yes. I mean no! Oh fuck, I don't know what I mean."

Mac turned his tongue sideways, running it along her slit. She was dripping wet now, emitting her sweet nectar. She'd be emitting an even sweeter taste as soon as she began to orgasm. He'd never known another woman capable of doing that.

"Oh baby..." Her fingers reached down to clutch at his head.

He warmed at the term of endearment. Pushing his tongue in deeper, he rewarded her with the feeling of his tongue rubbing along her vaginal wall. At the same time, he kept up his erotic attack on her clit. She began to shudder, her muscles stiffening in readiness. She was crying out, signaling her imminent explosion.

Here was where the fun began...

Mac took her to within a heartbeat of climax before withdrawing his tongue. "What do you need to say, Minarra?"

Minarra groaned in ultimate frustration. "I need to come...you asshole."

"That's not how we talk to the man who's giving us pleasure," he shook his head gravely. "Not at all."

She struggled to get free. "This is not funny, Mac."

Mac gave two licks, lazy and strategically placed between her parted, puffy lips. She wriggled a little more and then fell limp, the strength drained from her.

"What do you need to say?" He repeated.

Her glare said it all. "I hope this is getting you off," Minarra declared. "Because it's hell on me."

"I'm waiting," he ran his finger over her left nipple, bringing it to obedient attention."

"Please," she relented. "Please, let me come."

"How about, 'Please, Master.'" He tried to keep a straight face.

"How about jumping off the top of the nearest pyramid?" She growled.

"That's a very naughty slave girl," he teased, turning her over onto her side for a nice little ass pinching.

"Ouch, that hurts, you prick!"

"That's Master Prick to you." Mac pinched and caressed simultaneously, his motions designed to win quick surrender.

"Okay, okay..." she yielded to the heat he was generating. "I give. Please may I come...*Master*."

Mac moved quickly now, sinking his cock deep inside Min's scorching opening. "Yes," he said, their bodies belly to belly. "Come for me."

Minarra needed no further invitation. There was wonder in her eyes, release and deep, teeth-clenching lust. The idea of climaxing like this, by voice command was a powerful turn-on for her, just as it was for him. He held her tightly, even as he allowed himself to let go.

For the first time in his life, Mac did not feel in control. Neither did he feel used. Rather, it was a partnership, both of them enjoying a pleasure they'd generated together and which belonged to them equally. Sensations racking his body, linking their nerves and bones though press of flesh, fluids mixing, his own eruption matching her swirling release, a primal mix of energy and moisture and heat. And feelings, emotions conveyed through their touch. It was these extra elements of connection that transformed the act from mere sex to making love.

There was rhythm, motion and countermotion, a knowing of each other...the ignition of memories, deep in their souls that could never be forgotten. All this was there, latent in each other's eyes, the twisting and passion, the possibilities, from the moment they'd encountered one another in Malcolm's office.

It had to lead to this. Just as soon, all too soon, it would lead to another separation. For now, there was the timeless reward of lust—the ascension, spiraling upward around the edge of the volcano, and the mutual plunging in. Hot lava, burning, consuming and renewing. Limbs locked, fingers desperately clutching, mouths breathing for one another, hearts indistinguishable, one leaving off seamlessly where the other began. Blood pumping, explosions of ecstasy.

There was no getting up afterwards. Exhausted, they clung to each other, fighting off the darkness that seemed suddenly to descend upon them. Everything seemed so silent now. Had the whole city gone to sleep, or were they merely sunk too deep in each other's worlds?

For once he would not lie in a bed wondering, hoping that she was okay. For once, he had some say in the matter. He could, if need be, fight for her. And die.

To really protect her though, in the long run, he'd have to find a way to stay close to her. Always.

There was one way. One solution. Up to now he'd not dared to think of it. It involved a change in both their statuses, and it centered on a single, dreaded life-changing word.

To put it in a nutshell, Mac Macallister, confirmed hunk bachelor and Mummy Hunter, was thinking of proposing marriage.

Minarra was saying something about going to sleep. He couldn't really follow. He remembered holding her that much tighter and reassuring her that she was safe with him.

After that he fell asleep, more at peace than he'd felt in years. He had his purpose now. He was doing something…for her.

* * * * *

Minarra was in Mac's arms, her head on his powerful chest. Her mind was telling her not to fall asleep, because of the dreams that might come, but her limbs were so heavy. Like lead. Besides, she felt so safe with this man. No matter what he'd done to her relationship-wise, he'd never let harm come to her. He cared—in his own narrow way—he still cared. A man did not make love like that unless he felt something. She was sure of it, despite the fact that she had no experience to go on. It was instinct, just a feeling gleaned from the way he touched her. Despite the teasing, the pushing, the denial, underneath there was boundless respect for her.

From other women, she'd learned men could behave very differently, and often did. Apparently, the loving kind were few and far between. Even her father, for all his passion and desire to protect Minarra's mother had never truly been able to love Sofia. He'd blamed himself for that, along with everything else, but it was just his nature. There was no malice or cowardice in him. He would have given his life for Sofia, if only he'd known the suicide was coming.

These and other thoughts swirled in her mind, winding down, in tune with Mac's heartbeat. She was lulled, sated, catatonic and ready to give in to the sleep she so desperately needed.

* * * * *

That's it...don't fight it...

Minarra tried to reopen her half-closed eyes to see who was talking to her. Before she could react, however, she felt a hand on her arm. There was a flash of light and she was standing upright in the desert. A plain of pure-white crystal sand, specked with gems of every color. Above, the sun shone bronze, and the sky was a pale green.

The white-robed man with the shadowed, unreadable face was beside her, and for some reason she had this odd sensation that it was her father underneath that hood. When she reached to pull it down over his shoulders, however, he pushed back her hand, redirecting her to the horizon.

She saw the city, the one she went to in her dreams. A feeling of dread overcame her. She shook her head, wanting to run away. The man held her fast, his bony fingers clamping her wrist. Minarra realized now that she was naked and very vulnerable.

"Daddy?" She said.

At once lightning cracked across the bizarre, artificial landscape and the scene shifted. She was back in the throne room, Komen-tah beside her. He was wearing a black silk robe, open to the waist with a black girdle drawn about his middle. He was barefoot, his mighty biceps circled with gold bands. The whole of his head was decorated, carefully painted with symbols of the gods.

"Welcome home, my dear," he smiled smoothly, inclining his head. "I trust you are prepared?"

"Prepared for what?" She demanded.

Komen-tah laughed.

"Who brings this woman?" Thundered a voice, echoing high in the golden chamber.

The white-robed man released Minarra and bowed. Komen-tah took her hand, grinning. Suddenly Minarra understood the significance.

It was a wedding. Her wedding.

"No," she cried.

Chains appeared, heavy shackles binding her wrists and ankles, and another on her throat. She was wearing a gown of pale pink gauze, virtually see-through. The chains held her fast, making it impossible to lift her arms or legs. The white-robed man vanished and in his place a black-robed one appeared.

"Who takes this bride?" The voice inquired.

Now there was a red-robed man, standing directly in front of them, occupying the place of a minister or priest. Komen-tah leaned in close to Minarra, wrapping his arm tight around her waist.

"Aren't you happy, my dear?" He inquired. "You are to wed a god..."

She opened her mouth, but nothing came out.

Komen-tah was laughing even harder, sliding his hand over her ass. Minarra was squirming in vain.

"Hear ye, hear ye," said the man in the red robe.

Minarra drew a breath in horror. The voice was her father's. But as he took down his hood, she beheld not the face of Roger Hunt, but her own.

She watched her lips moving, pronouncing the marriage. "By the power vested in me by the god, Komen-tah, I hereby declare you—"

This couldn't be happening, not even in a dream.

"Yes," said Komen-tah, "it could."

Now Komen-tah had her face, too. She watched the slave girls crawl to her feet and kiss up her legs. They wanted between her thighs…they wanted to touch. Minarra blinked and now they were vipers, snakes, looking to fuck her. Her scream was silent, deep underwater. She was drowning…again. In the fluids of her own pussy, enough to fill the throne room, the whole of the city…

* * * * *

Hands on her shoulders pulled her up just in time. It was Mac, calling to her from the waking world. He was leaning over her, concern etched into his features. Impulsively she grabbed his neck, pulling him close.

"It's just a nightmare," he promised. "It's all over."

If only it were over that easily, she thought grimly.

He held her for a long time, until she stopped shaking. It had been a close call this time. She'd nearly died there, in the city. Would that have been the end of her? Would she have been lost to the world of sanity, the way her mother had?

Is that what Shera-Sa represented ultimately—a mad dream? Was that what her father had seen in the desert lights—his own mental destruction? Or was there something more to this...the odd coincidence of a map showing up, after eons of mystery. And with it these dreams, more vivid than waking life.

Whatever was going on, she could not sleep. Not until the mystery was solved. Mac would hear none of this, however.

"You're getting your rest, darling. And that's final."

She lacked the strength to fight...she could not even explain the dangers. His will, his soothing hands and words were too much to fight.

"I'll lie down with you. You'll see, it will be fine," he said.

Mac put her down on her side, spooning from behind. Complete and utter symbiosis. I could die like this, she thought, skin-to-skin, life forces in total harmony.

And perhaps tonight, I shall...

Chapter Five

Mac awoke to the slap of a pillow over his face. He looked up in sleepy bewilderment. It was Minarra and she was poised to strike again. Apparently he was out of her good graces again. "Min, what gives?" He croaked.

"I slept last night," she said, as though it were some great crime. "And you let me."

Mac snatched the pillow from her hand and tossed it over her head. "That is what people do at night," he pointed out.

"I told you not to let me," she accused. "And you didn't listen."

"But why shouldn't you sleep?"

"It doesn't matter. The point is that you ignored my wishes."

"Min, you're not making any sense," he complained.

"I don't have to," she said crossly. "I just have rights, that's all."

Mac licked his lips. Min was nude, her hair tousled. He wanted her badly. "How about we just fuck instead of arguing?" he proposed.

She shook her head. "You're pitiful, you know that? You think everything's about sex?"

He rubbed the back of his neck, thinking. "Well, maybe not *everything*."

"You're impossible," she rolled her eyes. "I'm going to take a shower, and I don't want to be disturbed."

Mac's cock thickened under the sheet. "You have two choices, Min. Either come back to this bed and take your lovemaking like a woman or I will drag you back and give it to you like the naughty little wench you are."

She tossed back her hair, walking away saucily. "I'm ignoring you Seth. As far as I'm concerned, we are colleagues, and that's it."

He grinned, recognizing the lilt in her voice. It was the playful Min...somehow he'd brought her back. Jumping from the bed, he intercepted her halfway to the bathroom. She was laughing and squealing as he swung her around into his arms. She felt so goddamn good this way, her lips opening to him, her body molding against him. There was no mistaking his erection between them, not to mention the peaks of her nipples.

"I assume you expect me to take care of this?"

He looked down at the pulsing shaft, which at the moment was poking her belly. "You are responsible for getting it into this state," he pointed out.

"Me?" She arched an eyebrow. "What the hell did I do—other than breathe?"

"That's all it takes. That's all it ever took."

She made a little cooing noise, laying her head on his shoulder. He'd said the right words.

Stroking her hair, he said, "I need you, Min. And not just your body. I need your heart, too..." His heart was thundering. The words, like it or not, were about to come spilling out. "Minarra, what I'm trying to say is...will you...will you consider marrying me?"

She pulled away from him, all tenderness and humor gone from her face. "What did you say? Never mind, I know what you said. I just can't... I can't believe it."

He stood frozen. There was no taking it back now. Hell, he wasn't even sure where it had come from exactly. Was he losing his mind here?

"Tell me why," she demanded. "Why would you want to marry me? After all these years?"

"Isn't it clear? How well we're matched? Even back then—"

"Never mind any of that, Mac. You told me once you loved me. Was that true? Is it true now?"

The words stuck in his throat. He owed her more than just a pat answer. "Min, there are things you need to know."

"No. I don't need to know anything. You already told me the answer.

Mac frowned. She was taking steps backward, toward the bathroom. "You had no right to ask me that," she declared. "No right to even...think it. And if you ever so much as *look* like you're going to do that again, I will find a way to cut you off completely from this expedition. Is that clear?"

"Of course." He kept his voice flat, a block of stone. "Your wishes will be respected."

She laughed sarcastically. "How big of you...now if you'll excuse me, I'm going to shower. Kindly hide that before I come out."

"Not a problem."

For some reason his acquiescence only seemed to aggravate her. Calling him a couple of choice names, she stormed off and slammed the door. Mac could hardly argue with her at this point. What the hell right *did* he have, after all this time, to try and ride back in like the cavalry, acting like nothing had happened between them to split them apart.

The trouble was that the split had everything to do with her father. The man whose memory she idolized more than anything in the world. How could he disturb that memory? Besides, what use was it now to blame another man for his actions? He could have said no to Roger but he hadn't. How could he go back and make something right that never would be?

His only option was to forget it all...

Finding his gun, he checked to make sure it was in working order. There was no telling what use he'd have for it out in the desert. After that he gave Hassan a call.

"What are you doing up so early, you son of a whore?" Hassan asked.

"I'm earning a living," he quipped. "Which is more than I can say for you."

Hassan laughed, rich and deep. "I don't have to earn a living, with men like you to cheat."

"I let you cheat me because I feel sorry for you. So is this expedition ready to go or not?"

"You need only say the word..."

"Consider it said."

"You're in a hurry then."

"The sooner the better, Hassan. Nothing personal, but this is a job I want over with ASAP."

"I'm surprised, my friend. If I were you, I'd want as much time with the little black-haired woman as possible."

"She's not my type," said Mac.

"Ahh…so the way is clear for me."

Mac felt his pulse quicken. "She's not yours, either," he said, a little too quickly. "She's not anyone's type."

Hassan paused, perhaps picking up on Mac's strong reaction. "If you say so…"

"I do." Mac hung up, put on his khaki shorts and pulled out a pack of cigarettes. Going to the wrought iron balcony, he leaned over the edge and looked down on the sordid, ancient city below. A city full of broken dreams and heartaches washed ashore on a mindless sea. A city full of ancient miseries and tragic secrets. A million unhappy endings, threadbare fairy tales worn to the level of mere survival. Existence, one sunrise to the next. One smoke-filled breath to the next.

He took a long drag off the unfiltered Turkish blend he'd picked up in Islamabad last month. He'd been to Porto Sayeed dozens of times but never before had he understood it or felt its pain. Not until now.

* * * * *

Minarra cried herself dry in the shower. Sitting against the wall of the small stall, knees drawn to her chest, the water splashing her knees and head and arms. A mindless sting, endless and unforgiving.

It wasn't fair. Where the fuck was that marriage proposal six years ago? When it would have meant something? When she could have acted on it.

All right, so she would have freaked out back then. And there would have been her father to consider. He was protective as a hawk. No man was ever good enough for her in his eyes, least of all an archeologist. Ironically, the more a man was like himself, the less Roger Hunt trusted him. And Mac was like him in spades. That's why they'd connected so easily.

Okay, so marriage six years ago would have seemed strange...awkward. She was just having fun with Mac. That summer was paradise, all the feelings and thrills and romance she'd missed in her life up to then. If only she'd known she'd never have it again.

In any event, Mac was doing nothing now but throwing a monkey wrench into the machinery of her life, her career. Wasn't it messy enough they'd ended up back in bed together? How bizarre was it that they could still have such incredible sex, even better than before, with so much tension between them.

Damn it, why did he have to come back into her life at all? Why did Malcolm have to pick him to lead this expedition? Why had her father made the man promise to watch over her? Better still, why did Daddy have to die at all? Why did he have to leave her with the burden—the curse of Shera-Sa? Well this would be the end of it. This would be the last expedition. Either this map would produce concrete proof of the city's existence or she would abandon her attempts to find it forever.

No more sixteen-hour days combing through ancient records, no more fighting tooth and nail for grants and academic respect for something no one in their right mind believed in. No more bizarre dreams brought on by overwork, or whatever the hell else was causing her to be swallowed up like this. And above all, no more Mac Macallister. Not in her present, not in her future. His ghost would be laid to rest, along with all the others.

Then she could reclaim her life. For the first time she could explore herself. Find her identity. Maybe even change her name. No more Minarra...no more Komen-tah.

This last thought produced a ringing noise in her head. An angry sound, something wanting to be heard, refusing to be denied. Something ancient and evil that would no longer live only in dreams or human imagination. She covered her ears. Looking up, she saw the water turn red. A cascade of blood about to hit her head. She screamed.

* * * * *

From reflex, Mac grabbed the gun. He was at the bathroom door seconds after hearing the screams. Minarra had locked it from the inside. "Min, open up!" He pounded the door.

Either she couldn't hear him or she didn't want to respond. Tucking the gun into the back of his shorts, he squared his shoulder against the barrier keeping him from the woman he loved. The wood gave way with a sickening crunch. Mac felt nothing from the impact—he'd have time for the pain later.

He found Minarra in the shower. She was against the back wall, flailing her arms. He leaped in, instantly soaking himself from the shower spray. "Baby, what's wrong?"

"B-b-bloo—" Her lips were blue. She was shivering, trying to say something.

Was she trying to say blood?

He gathered her against his chest. Whatever the fuck this was, he'd deal with it. He'd kill it. He'd do something.

"Sweetheart, it's all right," he soothed. "I'm here. You're safe."

"Mac," she sobbed, her strength draining. "It was horrible. So much...blood everywhere."

Mac felt a chill down his spine. She'd been hallucinating...like her mother. "Min, it's all gone. Whatever it was, it's all gone. I swear to god."

Demons of the mind...the only thing a man can't fight with his hands, Mac thought grimly.

Min looked up into his face. "You don't understand..." She kissed him then. Maybe as an afterthought, or was it intended to help explain?

Mac's desire rose instantly to the surface. "Sweetheart, if you keep on like this I'm going to take you back to bed," he gave her fair warning. "Is that what you want?"

She nodded, slowly, but fiercely. "I need it. Fuck me, Mac...make it go away."

There was no making it to the bed now. Mac tore at his drenched clothing, pulling off each item until he was naked. Lifting her by the hips he impaled her. Her sex was hotter, slicker than he'd ever remembered. Hissing in dark delight, eyes closed, she wrapped her legs around him, locking her ankles.

"Yes, baby," she encouraged, circling her arms around his neck. "Take me...fucking have me..."

Mac was not gentle this time, nor slow. He was a piston, cock pounding at her, slamming her ass cheeks against the tile. She cried out, egging him on. "Yes..." The word stretched into grunting syllables, laid one upon the other. Her pelvis was like a magnet, drawing him in, thrust after thrust. It was as hot as any sex they'd had in the desert — hotter even — and faster with all the fury and anguish bottled up over the years. Her nails dug into his shoulders. He was squashing her breasts, not wanting a single millimeter between them. She was like an itch, deep under his skin. Her breathing said it all, a cadenced "fuck me" noise that made it all just perfect. He didn't slow down for a second. Locking his teeth, he tightened his ass muscles, made one last magnificent drive and came. She cried out a whimper of joy and anguish.

Minarra came for him, like a wildcat, wound up and unleashed, claws bared, fangs sunk deep—the quintessential fur-covered predator, lusciously tamed in her lover's arms.

Their come mixed, mingling as it dripped with the water. They held onto one another through the storm, riding the crest of the waterfall, down into the rapids below. Washing themselves away, to a glorious, unspeakable sunset.

Eventually, Mac was able to turn off the water. "You're going home," he told Minarra, who was shivering in the corner.

She looked at him, about as formidable as a drowned cat. "No," she said fiercely, her eyes conveying the Hunt willpower. "You're taking me to Shera-Sa."

"You're going home," he repeated, though he knew he could never do that. In spite of his worst fears for her safety, he would take her, because she would accept nothing else. Truthfully, he'd be disappointed if she ever did. That was what made her so difficult, so incredible...so Minarra.

"I need a towel," she said.

He handed it to her. God, he wished he knew what made her tick, what the hell she needed and what it was that terrified her so.

Mac knew the history—Sofia's untimely end. *I couldn't handle the mother, you can't handle the daughter*, such was Roger's supreme impervious logic. He wasn't worthy—not for anything more than this. Roger had made that clear.

Mac went over the final checklist in his mind. Men, guns, food, water, archeological equipment, camp supplies, and more guns. That should about do it. And maybe some wooden crosses, too. To mark any graves they would have to dig.

Chapter Six

Minarra knew she would like Hassan the minute she saw that the big man was intent on needling Mac for the entire journey. He was one of those good-natured men, jolly and fun-loving, though she was quite glad she was not someone he considered an enemy. With all that muscle power and his quick eyes, she was quite sure he would make a deadly opponent.

She was less certain about the other men, though she'd leave them to Hassan and Mac to keep in line. Hassan had already made it clear that should any of his deputies so much as look askance at her or say a disrespectful word, he would happily dispatch them "a few years earlier to their Great Maker, Allah."

As for Mac, he would do the same, she was sure. As a matter of fact, the expedition leader had become so protective since leaving the hotel she was starting to feel claustrophobic. Not to mention paranoid.

It didn't help that their convoy looked more like a military invasion than a scientific expedition. All three of the jeeps were fitted with mounted machine guns along with a rocket launcher and a box of AK-47's in the Land Rover.

"It's all precautionary," the tight-lipped Mac said, helping her into the Rover.

Hassan had offered for her to ride in one of the jeeps with him, but Mac had refused — a bit brusquely, in her opinion.

"It is quite all right," the big-hearted Hassan assured her. "He wants your protection, in case of trouble, you will make sure he doesn't get hurt, won't you?"

She grinned in response to his wink. "Absolutely," she assured him.

As soon as the convoy was underway, Mac wanted to hear more about the vision-dreams. She would never forgive herself for having reacted so foolishly in the shower, because now her secret was out and the man would treat her like a hysterical, helpless female.

"I already told you everything I know," she said curtly. "It's no big deal. Just stress."

"Stress might give you headaches or even dizzy spells," he lectured. "But it does not generally cause a person to see blood pouring from a shower nozzle."

Minarra tied back her hair against the light wind whipping through the open cab of the jeep. Admittedly, the experience in the shower had been the most frightening of her life. It really had looked and felt like blood...

* * * * *

She hid her face, cowering, terrified of having the vile substance on her body. At first it burned like fire, like the sting of Mac's spanking hand multiplied by a hundred, like the bee sting she'd gotten as a little girl, multiplied by a thousand.

She thought her flesh was going to melt off. But just as quickly as the agony had come, it left. She was standing, covered in sand, in the middle of a vast dune. The sand was black, like the dusted granules of an ancient volcano. Strange lightning erupted across the sky, little zigzags off bigger ones, purple, electric-blue and red.

There was no sun but she sky was lit a hazy, vague orange. With her peripheral vision, she could see rushing shapes, too quick to grasp in her mind's eye. Strange objects littered the desert, huge pieces of artificial material, neither metal nor plastic. They were of all shapes, tubes and cones, intricate semispheres cracked open. Like some kind of supertech junkyard.

The lightning was starting to hit the ground, and as it did, she could make out flashing scenes, like shimmering movie images. Civilizations passed before her eyes, working backward from the present. All the way back through the Middle Ages, to Greece and Rome and Egypt...

At a certain point the lightning was matched by thunder. Her heart raced. She knew what was coming next. Shera-Sa. The proto-city was about to rise again.

The earth beneath her began to rumble. The vibrations shook her teeth. In the pit of her stomach she felt a wrenching. Something was wrong here. She felt a tugging at her ankle. Looking down, she saw a skeletal hand grabbing her ankle. Minarra screamed as another hand grabbed her other ankle. More and more skeletons were emerging, headfirst from the sand.

A trumpet blared, an unholy, bleak wail. The skeletons were forming ranks, taking on flesh and armor. An army was rising. At the same time, she saw the walls, white as ivory, strong as diamond. The ramparts of Shera-Sa. First and greatest city of them all.

Mother of civilization…coming to reclaim her children.

She could see a troop of horses in the distance. At the lead was Komen-tah, leading his cavalry. In his hand, above his head, he held a flaming weapon, more than a sword and as bright as any star. The others held weapons too, and Minarra realized that they were on their way to conquer the nations. Shera-Sa would rule the world of this day as it had the ancient world.

Her mind willed it to stop. Visions overwhelmed her of a terrible, bloody war to come, the worst the world had ever seen, millions of refugees, whole continents laid to waste, and in the end, all humans paying homage to the mad prince.

And his consort.

Minar-ra…her namesake…

* * * * *

But it hadn't happened yet. They were waiting for something. They needed something, and it had to do with the modern Minarra. Indeed, Minarra realized now that the ancient priestess and her lover had been trying to break into her mind all this time. They wanted to lure her to Alcazara. They might even have planted the map.

What exactly did they want, though? And why plant the dreams? Were they trying to make her feel trapped in the past? How would it serve their ends to drive a single archeologist mad with unbearable visions?

She had been about to confront the old Minar-ra when Mac awoke her, coming to her rescue. Mostly she was grateful to him, though a part of her wished she could have seen. Would it be like looking in a mirror—as in her last vision? Or was there some other horror in store for her?

The answers lay out there, in the desert. But also in her own past. Could it be there was more than mere coincidence involved in her naming? Had her father known something he'd not shared? Had he seen more than he'd revealed, even on his deathbed?

For now, she had no choice but to rely on Mac. The one man who cared most for her in the world, and who had the oddest ways of showing it. Running off and leaving her for six years, then storming back in, wanting to be her savior...and now her husband.

"Why won't you trust me?" he asked, placing a hand on her thigh. "I can't help if you don't share."

She shivered at his touch on her bare skin. She should never have worn shorts out here. "Please, Mac," she stiffened. "I'd prefer you don't..."

"Don't what? Show my feelings? I'm sorry for being human, Min." Mac put his hand back on the wheel. He sounded angry...hurt even.

"I appreciate the concern," she replied in as neutral a tone as possible. "But if you don't mind. I'd like to get a little rest."

Mac drove on in silence. She let the road lull her into a state of semiconsciousness. If only he knew how grateful she was to have him beside her. He could never know this, but she did not know if she could bear to be without him right now.

They stopped for a break about two hours outside of the city. The road ahead was a shimmering mess, the superheated air creating a mirage effect. As far as the eye could see there was nothing but broken stone and small tough, weeds. On the horizon was the back end of the dunes. By morning they would be in the Belly of Gehenna, the aptly named desert valley that comprised the center of this ancient land.

They would encounter few if any vehicles and little in the way of permanent civilization. It was here they would find Shera-Sa, if it existed. They would navigate by the stars, and by the measurements of Shera-Sa's mathematicians. Minarra wanted and hoped for much more. She would follow the footsteps of explorers down through the centuries, hoping the fabled city lay somewhere buried, preserved by the sand, waiting to be rediscovered, to be reawakened to a new dawn.

What mysteries would Shera-Sa hold in her temples and palaces? What wonders to spark the modern mind? It boggled the mind to think that all doubt about the city's existence would finally be destroyed. And yet, given the frightening nature of Minarra's dreams, she also had reason to hope it would all prove to be a hoax after all.

"We'll camp behind that ridge," Mac pointed, about a half hour before sunset.

The western sky was a glowing, baked orange, layered with ancient reds. This was no sky of the New World, no sky that could ever hang over a modern city or town. It was a sky fit for fortune-tellers and flying carpets. And maybe a winged, sandaled god or two.

Minarra said nothing, preferring to keep a judicious silence. Mac waved the convoy off the road, gathering the vehicles into a loose, yet defensive circle. Hassan hopped from his Rover, his AK-47 in tow and began shouting orders. He was quite a sight, in his desert boots, gathered Bedouin style pants and vest. He looked at home here, as much as any human could.

Gathering her things, Minarra set them down on the ground. It was her intent to help set up the tents, but Mac refused to allow it.

"Sit there," he said harshly, directing her to a folding chair. "I don't want you exerting yourself."

"For heaven's sake," she complained. "I'm not pregnant."

She could only imagine what the man would do if she was.

"You just worry about the map," he said. "Let us do the grunt work."

Hassan laughed. "You sound like a married couple!"

Minarra felt a tiny stab. Was it that obvious that there was a history…a thing between them? Surely it wasn't something akin to a marriage relationship, though. Was it?

"I wouldn't wish that on any woman," said Mac wryly, hiding his emotions as deftly as ever. "I do the gender a favor by staying a bachelor."

"You don't fool me," Hassan slapped his shoulder. "You're a man in love. You have been since the day I met you and one day you will tell me who she is."

"You talk too much," Mac grumbled, directing him to the outer perimeter. "The sun is about to set and we've barely gotten started here."

Minarra's heart thudded in her chest. Mac in love? But with whom? What other woman had come into his life? And why hadn't he married her? Was another woman the reason he'd left her six years ago? Damn it, why wouldn't he just be honest with her and stop sending her these ridiculous mixed messages?

Whoever said women were complicated and mercurial had obviously never looked inside the mind of your garden variety male, she mused. Pulling out the map and an accompanying notepad, she set about marking the day's progress.

They were on the way. Within a day or two…finally.

This one will be for you, Daddy…

* * * * *

Mac had a very bad feeling in his gut. Maybe the worst ever. Something bad was going to happen. Looking for Shera-Sa was one of those accursed quests. The kind of obsession that eats a man's life and bleeds bad luck, staining all the people he loves and touches. Roger Hunt was one such example, but there'd been others before him. Sir Edward Mathison, the nineteenth-century explorer who'd gone mad in the desert and returned to England only to lose his fortune and his family in a series of freak accidents. Farrouk of Algeria, who'd been set upon by rats and eaten alive and most recently, the final king of Alcazara, who'd mounted seven expeditions before his assassination.

If only Minarra had accepted his proposal. If only she had let him take her away to some beautiful island for a secret wedding and a quiet honeymoon. He couldn't blame her for refusing, though. Why should she trust his motives? He didn't understand them himself.

Besides, no man, or woman could fight destiny. And theirs led here.

Had they been meant for happiness, they'd have united in the beginning and had a little family, pursuing a pleasant career at some Ivy League school, teaching the archeologists of the future and venturing occasionally into the field.

Those dreams were a bad omen, make no mistake. He wasn't a superstitious man, but even the most scientific of explorers had to be a little creeped out by some of the things that had happened to the various unearthers of ancient tombs over the years. Mummy's curses, odd diseases, latent ghost traps. Masses of mysterious energy. He'd made a mint selling these ideas on television. Personally, he had never cared if he offended any supernatural powers that be. What did a man have to lose who had no love in his life?

But now he had Minarra back—at least under his temporary care—and so he had everything to lose. He didn't like the look of her at all. She was pale. She was glassy-eyed. She was covering up just how bad all of this was. His every instinct was to protect, to distract, and to wrap her as tight as he could.

Naturally, she was suspicious, if not downright hostile. All through dinner—falafel and bread heated over a crackling fire—she'd avoided his company in favor of Hassan. He'd have been jealous had he not known that Hassan would never make a move on anyone in his crew. He was just too much of a gentleman that way.

And Minarra was a lady. She had no intention of seducing or even flirting with Hassan. She simply wished to keep clear of Mac—a man, a situation in which she felt compromised. Steering a wide berth around her, he tended to camp business, checking vehicle engines, adding fuel and organizing the night watch schedule. Minarra spent a little time by the fire and went to bed alone, in her own tent.

Mac, meanwhile, had pretty much reconciled himself to a night alone. Volunteering to keep the fire going, he let Akbar hit the hay. A rifle by his side, a full pack of Turkish cigarettes in his pocket, he settled in by the fire to wait out the darkness. There was nothing like the silence of the desert to help a man sort out his thoughts. There was no lying to oneself out here. Not under these stars, sharp as scimitar points, laid out on a canvas of black velvet, your bottom resting on the endless sand, a timeless symbiosis, an ecosystem harsher and more beautifully brutal than any man could bear with the naked soul.

Maybe it was time to return to teaching, he thought. To try to pass on the few things he'd learned over the years. Maybe find a protégé to take under his wing, like Minarra's father had done for him. Hopefully the relationship would end up better. Mac would make sure not to have a beautiful daughter for him to fall in love with—that would help.

He took a drag off the half-spent cigarette. Who the fuck was he kidding? He didn't have it in him to stand in front of a lecture hall and spout dry science. He was a field man. An action junkie. Besides, any classroom would be full of young women to remind him of Minarra. That would be a pain worse than death. To look at all those eyes, eager and pretty, all the while thinking of the one and only woman who ever really meant a damn thing to him.

No, he wasn't meant to be a professor.

From here on in, he decided, he'd be spending his social time with mummies. And cutthroats, at whatever hellhole bars he could find to get drunk at in between expeditions. It wasn't the most original plan for forgetting a woman, but then again, sometimes the tried and true methods were the best.

* * * * *

"Do you think you will find it?" Asked Hassan, quietly announcing his presence over Minarra's shoulder.

She shrugged, still very much engaged in the map. It had become her friend by now, her constant companion. In a way, her lover. "Many have looked," she replied, knowing that Hassan himself had sought the fabled city at one point in his life. "People far better than I."

"And many who are far worse. May I sit?"

She nodded.

"Thank you." He took up a place across from her, legs crossed beneath him. He was a man who seemed comfortable in any position, anywhere. Clearly, with those deep eyes of his, that centered countenance, there was more to him than just the mercenary and guide he was purported to be.

"Why did you agree to help Mac?" She asked, somewhat impulsively.

He smiled, elusively. "You mean given that I myself have already failed in finding Shera-Sa?"

"I meant no offense."

"None taken. I have passed the point of attaching my own happiness to earthly accomplishments. Our successes choose us and not the other way around."

"That sounds fatalistic."

"Not when one considers the need for intense preparation to meet that which may come our way," he countered. "Love for instance. One's destiny is shaped by how one faces it."

"I have no use for love." She stiffened.

"You think yourself too strong," he said, nodding. "Or too young...or too old. Perhaps you even dismiss yourself as too weak. But it does not matter. It comes nonetheless. Just as Shera-Sa will come to you...if the city chooses."

"Has Mac ever talked about me?" She wanted to know.

"He does not speak to me of personal things."

"Well he must have dropped some clue. He asked me to marry him, for heaven's sake. We haven't even seen each other in years. And the last time...well, it wasn't exactly a parting to leave a woman eager for more."

Hassan pursed his lips. His eyes were dancing in the moonlight, as though some very ancient merriment were plucking the heartstrings of his soul. "He is afflicted by love, Miss Hunt. You know that as well as I. These and all the other questions you have—for him, for Shera-Sa—they have answers in only one place. And you alone know where that place is."

"I don't know anything," she sighed, rising to her feet. "I think I'll just go to bed."

She paused to give him a peck on the cheek. "Thank you," she said.

"For what?" Asked Hassan.

"For being Mac's friend."

* * * * *

"Is this seat taken?"

Mac looked up, momentarily taken aback. It was Min, wrapped in an army blanket against the mild chill — unusual for this climate, to say the least.

He moved the rifle across his lap. "Be my guest."

She sat about six inches away. Close, but not touching. "How long have you been smoking?" She asked.

"Since...a while ago." He'd been about to say since her father's funeral, the day he'd lacked the guts to talk to her, going instead to a nearby liquor store and gas station, obtaining a bottle of whiskey and a pack of cigarettes, in that order. "You want one or are you still habit free?"

"I have other addictions. Anyway, those look more like rolled tar sticks."

"Are you kidding? These are tame, by Turkish standards," he quipped. "Only old women smoke this brand."

Minarra laughed lightly and then turned her attention to the fire. She looked preoccupied, older than she had since he first saw her in Malcolm's office. "Mac," she said, after a few moments' pause. "About this morning..."

"No," he cut her off. "No explanations. Let's just leave it. Please."

She sighed. "All right. Can I ask you something, then?"

"Sure. As long as you don't make me promise up front to answer."

"How come you never talked to me about your childhood?"

"Not much to say. The usual things...skinned knees, baseball leagues, prom dates."

"But your life wasn't usual at all. Daddy told me a couple of things. He said... He said you barely knew your parents."

Mac's jaw set. The tension was old, reflexive. "He shouldn't have said anything at all."

Her hand slipped over to his, covering the knuckles, which at the moment were laying over the stock of the rifle. "Why are you ashamed, Mac? None of us are responsible for the things that happen to us as children."

"Sure," he retorted with a cynicism she did not deserve. "We're all clean slates, right? I prefer the ancient view—we're all born fucked on account of every screwup made by our ancestors, every stinking generation of them."

"You can't really believe that?"

"Sure I can. Look what I did to you. That will live on in my children and their children. If I ever have any, that is."

"You want to make me angry," she decided. "You're always doing that—trying to make me feel some emotion, trying to push my buttons. Just once, can't you let your guard down?"

"There's nothing to see under there, Min. The lights are out and no one's home."

"You told me before that you wanted to give an explanation about your leaving. What if you start there?"

He pulled out another cigarette, along with a silver flask, half-filled with whiskey. He kept it for special occasions. Whenever he needed a little anesthesia. "I said there *was* an explanation," he held out the flask. "I never said I wanted to give it."

Minarra took a swig and handed it back. "You've turned into a coward," she pronounced, with uncharacteristic bluntness.

"That's where you're wrong, Min. I always was a coward. I just hid it, there in your father's shadow. You want to know something about me? Fine. My father was a second-rate boxer, a drunkard who earned his living breaking bones for the Irish mob. When he wasn't attacking my mother. When I was six, he was shot dead in front of me by one of my mother's brothers. He was protecting her, standing over her prone body, trying to keep my father from beating her any more. My uncle went to jail because he couldn't afford a lawyer to get him off and my mother ended up in a mental hospital with a nervous breakdown. The state stepped in and I spent the next twelve years doing the foster home shuffle."

"Mac...I had no idea."

"It doesn't mean a thing," he shrugged. "Everybody's got a tough luck story. You can't let it rule you, that's all."

"You're not everybody," she squeezed his hand.

"So who am I?" He asked, deciding to turn the tables. "Seems to me I'm not the only one keeping his guard up lately. "Am I someone special to you or not?"

The hand retracted. She was pulling back, like a scared rabbit. "You'll always be in my heart, you know that."

"Actually, I don't know shit about what you think, Min." He pushed the smoldering tip of his latest, spent cigarette into the sand. "You know what the desert is?" he muttered. "It's one big, ocean wide, fucking ashtray."

"You're getting drunk, Mac."

"I should be so lucky," he took another gulp, hoisting the silver container skyward. It had been Roger's flask. Apparently, Minarra didn't recognize it. The old man had stashed it in with the supplies he'd packed for Mac, the morning of his exile. It had the initials RH and Mac often thought it was Roger's way of letting him feel connected, no matter what.

By the time Mac looked back down, Minarra was sniffling. Shit—now he was making her cry on top of everything else. "Min, I'm sorry," he rasped. "Jeezus—I'm such an ass."

She buried her head on his shoulder, choking back a sob. "No you're not. It's not you I'm upset with. It's the fucking...dreams. I can't sleep, I can't think."

He held her tightly. "It's okay, Min. We'll beat this, I promise."

"But it's not your fight."

He grasped her by the upper arms, looking her in the eye. "I'm making it my fight, you hear me?"

She nodded, her lower lip still trembling. He'd never seen her like this, so distraught. To think he might be adding to the stress with his own foolish proposal was more than he could bear.

"Just stay here with me by the fire," she said softly.

Mac let her nestle in, as close as she wanted. He knew she was terrified to sleep, but he also knew she would succumb, sooner or later. Sure enough, within a few minutes of watching the crackling blaze, lulled by the dancing orange shapes, warmed by their mutual body heat, she began to nod off.

He gripped the stock of the gun. He'd give anything in the world to get inside her head, to be able to deal with these demons, one-on-one. As it was, he was relatively helpless. Not a comforting feeling for a man who'd struggled all his life to be strong and independent, who'd worked ten times as hard as anyone else to overcome obstacles. From the time he'd known himself truly alone in the world to that fateful moment during a museum trip at school when he'd seen his first mummy, he had become a lone warrior, on a quest.

The day of that trip, as soon as school was over, he'd gone to the library. Finding every magazine he could, he'd devoured the information. Finally, he'd found Roger's picture on the cover of a magazine. Bearded, in khakis, the look of a true hero on his face. Mac had smuggled out the magazine. It had become his most treasured possession. He'd carried it to four more foster homes and then to college.

Eventually he would meet Roger Hunt in person, and apply for a job as his research assistant.

"Why should I hire you?" He'd inquired in his usual blunt manner, tossing the young man's scant application on his desk. "I have at least a half-dozen others better qualified than you."

That's when Mac had taken out the picture and handed it over.

Roger unfolded it, studying his own image. "I abhor sycophants," he said.

"I understand, sir."

"You'll work harder than you ever have in your life."

"I expect to."

He'd scowled roundly. It was an expression Mac would later understand as one of approval. If he didn't like you, you suffered far worse at the man's hands.

"Report tomorrow," Roger had ended the interview. "Eight a.m."

Thus had begun his work with the great archeologist.

Mac looked down to check on Min. She was nodding heavily, fighting the sleep she so desperately needed.

"Got to...stay awake," she mumbled, her sweet mouth slurring the words.

Her body was going limp. "Just let go, baby," he murmured, shifting his weight and moving the gun so she could lay her head in his lap.

Minarra purred like a kitten. Curling up her legs, the blanket underneath her, she snuggled against him. Mac's heart swelled. Such a simple act of trust, and yet so very full, and warming to his soul.

"Sleep," he promised. "And let me keep guard over your dreams."

If Shera-Sa was out there, he'd find it. And if any ghosts or demons showed up, he would send them packing straight back to hell.

Or die trying.

Sometime later, Hassan came to relieve him.

"She pays you the highest honor," he noted, pointing out the sleeping woman.

"What honor is that?" Asked Mac, somewhere between skepticism and cynicism. "Pretending to like me in her sleep?"

"You miss the point, my friend. She came to you, in her time of deepest fear. She singled you out, she made herself completely vulnerable, trusting her body, her soul to you."

Mac swallowed. He hadn't looked at it that way. As usual, he'd been trying to push things another way, out of sheer stubbornness. As a result, he'd missed the bigger picture. She hadn't agreed to marry him, but maybe the reasons weren't what he thought. If that was true, then he was really in the dark. Helpless, for the first time in his life. "Hassan, I don't know what I'm going to do," he rasped. "I don't know if I can live without her."

Hassan's smile radiated peace, wisdom. "You are not living without her—she is right here. In your arms."

"But tomorrow…"

"What is tomorrow?" asked Hassan. "Can you see it or taste it? What do you know of it but shadows, ghosts in the brain? It is no more real than yesterday. Do you wish to live in dreams…or in reality?"

"You're right," said Mac. "Damn it, you are absolutely right."

Filled with determination, he lifted Minarra into his arms. She immediately and comfortably nuzzled his neck, her eyes still closed.

"I am taking her to her tent," he said. "You'll find me there."

"I won't look," Hassan said.

"I meant for emergencies. You'll know where to find me."

Hassan grinned. "The universe allows time for things such as this, my friend. You will not be interrupted."

"I believe you, Hassan. I don't know why, but I do." With that, he took her across the camp to her tent. To make love to her as she had never been made love to before.

* * * * *

Minarra stirred to gentle but firm whispers in her ear. "Min…I need you tonight. I have to be inside you… I have to have you…one last time."

Her senses came alive as Mac spoke to her. She was on her back, on her own bedroll. She'd fallen asleep outside. He'd brought her back here, to the safety of her tent. "Oh Seth." She spoke his name, reaching up with hungry, parched lips. "I need you, too. I never stopped…"

It was like a dream, a good one to counter all the disturbing visions of Shera-Sa. This was truly her own passion she was feeling, for a man she had chosen long ago. In a different lifetime, it seemed.

She felt her breath quicken, her body erupting with tiny pools of heat everywhere on the surface of her skin. He was undressing her, very slowly and reverently, but with a singularity of focus that bespoke his lust.

He wanted her…he had to have her. What bigger turn-on could there be for a woman?

She wished he'd started here, instead of proposing marriage. Their prior couplings had only stirred the old emotions, the old ambivalence. What she needed was a decisive possessing. By a man ready to show her how he'd changed.

He paused after removing her shirt, bra, shoes and socks.

"You're so beautiful, Min…your body…your breasts." His hand was cupping them, encircling the naked flesh.

She moaned softly, arching her back, hands overhead. "Mac," she cried softly. "Tie me…please?"

Mac moved expertly, smoothly, as though he'd anticipated the request all along. Lying alongside her, he extracted her canvas belt from its loops. Crossing her wrists, he wrapped them in the strip of canvas and secured them—deliciously snug, not painful. Testing the bond, she found it more than sufficient to hold her.

"Mac," she exhaled, her pussy creaming for him, "take me."

Leave me no choices...make me give in to the love I feel...make me trust.

Mac took off her shorts and her panties without further ado. After that, he simply took a moment to enjoy her nudity. She watched with glazed, fascinated eyes, her taut stomach clenched, nipples painfully exposed and swollen, a study in feminine anticipation. His to command.

Her captive fists clenched in wonderful helplessness as he took off his shirt. She wanted to kiss and lick every inch of that well-formed stomach and chest.

As it was she could do nothing but whimper. And offer herself...

Her breathing shot up another notch, to near panting as he undid his shorts, and pulled down the zipper. That luscious cock...she could eat it whole. Alternatively, she could kiss and worship it for days on end. The things it did to her...the way it had taken possession of her in the past. The way it ruled her fantasies. The way it had swept back into her life...starting this cycle all over.

And now here it was again, inches away. From her pussy. Her ass and mouth.

Mac leaned forward, tantalizing, his body coming toward her. Every part of her cried out in anticipation. Would it be his thighs? His pelvis? His pecs? Which would touch her first?

It was his hand, reaching for the belt, taking hold of it, thereby pinning her down. Minarra surged with hot, sexual weakness. The pleasure of consensual bondage. Taking her nipple in his mouth, he applied the flat of his hand like a vise, to open her legs.

He bit a little harder as she resisted. Minarra gasped, giving him what he wanted. He knew what he wanted, immediately pushing his knee between her thighs.

"Move against me," he ordered. "Hump my leg."

Her mouth opened in slight shock at the request, but she did as she was told. It felt good right away, a kind of sweet ache, a nasty delight as she rubbed her excited pussy against him. She felt so primal, so much like an animal, seeking to pleasure her soft body in such a way against the hardness of his muscles. And yet she could not resist the sensations that were building up and down her body.

He let her go on a few minutes until she was in the throes of passion. He then removed his knee, offering her instead his lips to kiss. She went for them, desperate. At this point she could and would take any form of contact with him, under any conditions. It was a matter of trust mixed with sheer lust. She sought his mouth with her tongue, though it was his tongue that took hold of her. She opened, deeper and deeper, wanting to pull him inside her through this and every orifice. Every part of him, subsumed within every part of her.

At last he broke the seal, and moved for something more elemental. Yes...his cock. He was going to put it inside her. He was going to pierce her.

And she was going to yield. Absolutely.

Mac sank his cock inside her, his body pressed atop hers, a perfect fit. She began to shiver at once, already yielding. He pulled himself back, and then returned to his place, his rightful place inside her. Again and again, he did this, his rhythm neither fast nor slow, neither harsh nor lax. She could not count the times, could not keep track of the seconds or even of her own heartbeats. There was only their mutual pulse, bodies clinging, communicating, generating heat and sweat, pure as the salt of the desert.

Mac made a single moaning noise, totally endearing and inspiring. His cock swelled to what felt like twice its normal size and then the semen came. A flood of it—pulsing and spurting inside her. She responded with an avalanche all her own, a falling down upon him, a waterfall. An oasis in the dunes, green with life and explosive with energy. The two of them clung to each other long past the climax, all the way down to the peaceful lethargy of sleep. The last thing she remembered, as she slipped away, sated and happy, was that this gorgeous, wonderful man who had just taken her to the moon had just recently asked her to marry him.

It seemed too good to be true. At least given her family history. Or could it be she was breaking the Hunt curse, preparing to find a destiny all her own? She had a peculiar feeling the answers would come soon. Whether she wanted them to or not.

Chapter Seven

Minarra awoke in a state of pure bliss. She sat up, stretching. The ground beneath her was cool to the touch, though she could feel the pink sunlight already heating the air.

Still tingling from Mac's touch, still feeling his hard cock inside her, feeling primal and wicked, lazy and sexy as a cat, she crawled across her sleeping bag to the entrance of her tent.

She wasn't sure how he'd done it, but his loving had kept the dreams at bay. Maybe he was just a good luck charm, or he had some kind of power, but either way she had ended up feeling better than she had in ages.

He was a naughty boy for leaving her, though, for making her wake up all alone. She'd tell him that, too, and maybe threaten to tie *him* down next time since he obviously had trouble keeping his butt in one place.

God, but it had been good, though. Every bit of tension was smoothed out of her. By binding her hands, in that one simple act, he'd allowed her to let go, to let him into all her secret pleasure places. And he knew them all, too. He could write the book on her. Publish the definitive map. Frankly, it was dangerous to have a man know that much about her pleasure. She might have to kill him yet…

Or make him love her again, suckling and nibbling, thrusting and teasing, lashing her with hot words, employing tongue and cock and above all his hands, everywhere alive and expressive. Damn, she was getting herself worked up again. She'd have to do something about that, wouldn't she?

Peeking through the flap, Minarra was treated to an unpleasant surprise. She saw the men moving rapidly, loading the vehicles. She rose to her feet, instantly tense. Mac was over by the lead jeep, fiddling with the big machine gun. His face was serious, no-nonsense.

"What's going on?" She asked.

"Bandits," he told her. "We need to move fast."

"Was anyone going to tell me?"

"I was waiting until the last minute. I didn't want to—"

"Worry me," she completed the sentence, a broken record by now. "Damn it, Mac, when are you going to stop treating me like some kind of china doll? I grew up with this kind of thing. I think I can handle myself fine."

He put his hand over her wrist as she reached into the big storage box for one of the automatic rifles. "What do you think you're doing, missy?"

She pulled her hand away. "I'm getting a gun, like everyone else. And don't call me 'missy'."

His frown was deep and ingrained. She did a double take, he looked so much like her father right then.

"You are not handling a gun. You are riding in this jeep and when the trouble comes, you will keep your head down and that's an order."

"Fine," she shot back. "I won't fight you anymore."

I'll just lull you into a false sense of security and then when the shooting starts, I'll hop right into the fray and do my part...

"I'll believe that when I see it," he grumbled. "Now get in."

"But my stuff…the map."

Mac cursed under his breath. "Get the map, leave the rest. Hurry!"

A man was shouting, running up from behind. Apparently whoever was after them was closing in fast. Minarra grabbed the attaché case, the map inside. She ran back to the jeep and hopped into the passenger seat. Everything was happening so fast. A few minutes ago, she'd been thinking about lovemaking, and now they were running for their lives.

"Those must be some bandits who can chase us away," she remarked. "Given all the firepower you brought."

Mac said nothing as he put the vehicle in gear. He was hiding something. She knew it.

"I have a right to know," she reminded him. "It's my neck like anyone else's."

"It's the rebels," he said tightlipped. "It appears they are heading this way, intending to make an assault on the capital. We have to push further into the desert, try and pass through their lines before they encircle us."

"Why not head back to the city for protection?"

"We'd never make it," he shook his head. "There's too many of them. Elements of the army are deserting to the other side—we didn't see this coming."

"I am taking a gun," she leaned over the seat, "and that's final."

He was in no position to stop her, occupied as he was navigating the jeep at full throttle over the ancient, cracked road. "Just make sure you point it in the right direction," he quipped.

"Keep lying to me, and it'll be straight at your head," she retorted.

Mac laughed. "I love you too, baby."

Minarra heard the pain in his voice, hidden below the bravado. Her rejection of his proposal had cut him to the quick, she could tell. It was a wound no amount of lovemaking could heal. So she'd truly succeeded, then, in hurting him as he had hurt her. Had that been her real aim—revenge? If so, she'd served it as a dish a little too cold even for her own liking.

The rest of the morning and afternoon was uneventful. They stopped only once, for the barest few minutes to relieve themselves and add gasoline to the vehicles. The whole time, they encountered only a few stray camels. It was eerily quiet. Minarra was not fooled for a minute that the danger had passed. She could feel it in the air—a kind of tension, growing, mounting.

Shortly before dusk, a trio of helicopters appeared, heading in their direction. They were the military transport variety, with troops inside leaning out the open doors with long, heavy weapons.

Minarra tensed, taking aim.

"It's all right," he touched her arm. "They're government forces. Headed back to the capital. They won't bother us."

She looked at the soldiers' faces, dark and haggard. From the looks of them, they were in full retreat. Not a very good sign. The blades thwacked in the hot dry air, momentarily cutting off verbal communication. Minarra concentrated on the feel of Mac's hand on her arm.

It was the most normal she'd felt all day.

Could she ask him to keep it there, see if he was willing to entwine his fingers in hers? Lord knew what he thought of her by now. Last night he'd said it was the last time they'd make love. Did he really mean that?

A feeling of loneliness, as shocking as it was deep, pervaded Minarra's heart as Mac let go of her and returned his fingers to the steering wheel. *Damn it*, she chided herself. *What a time for me to get emotional.*

"There's a good chance we'll die out here, isn't there?" She asked once the whirring machines were out of range.

"I don't want you thinking such things," he chastised.

"Damn it, Mac, you're doing it again," she called him on the carpet. "Treating me like a child."

"What do you expect, Min? You keep acting like one."

Her feelings of tenderness for the man spun in a heartbeat, to wrath. "Go to hell...you prick."

"You see? There's an excellent case in point," he used her own outburst against her. "Thank you for proving my argument."

Her mind went black, thinking of various forms of slow torture for the man. "Just don't talk to me anymore. Do us both a favor."

Oh fuck it. He was right. She was letting him get to her. Why was she so quick to lose her temper with this man? No one else had ever been able to get to her like this, not even her father. How was she supposed to fight back? She sat fuming, until the sun was a mere line drawn above the desert.

"We're going to keep driving all night," he told her a while later, breaking the silence between them. "We'll make a quick stop to refuel. You can tend to your feminine business, but you'll have to keep it to a minimum."

Feminine business...was there any limit to this man's gall? She was sitting here with a loaded machine gun, ready and willing to kill...and he wanted to write her off as some over-pampered priss?

"You have three minutes," he declared as they pulled over near a large dune, sometime after nightfall.

"Gee," she said in her best ditz imitation. "I hope that's enough time to paint my toenails."

He shone the flashlight in her face. "What the hell's gotten into you now, Min?"

"Nothing," she snapped, swinging her leg out of the jeep.

At least nothing that a two-by-four upside his head wouldn't cure.

Mac intercepted her at the back end of the jeep, blocking her path. "That's a load of crap, Min. Tell me what this is really about."

"Get the hell out of my way — it's my three minutes and I will spend them without you, thank you very much."

"You will tell me," he grabbed her upper arm. "That's an order."

Minarra winced. Why couldn't he be like other men and just not care whether she had feelings at all? Better still, why couldn't he shut up and just hold her and kiss her? What if this was their last chance? What if death was awaiting them over the next dune?

"You really want to know?" She replied, sick and tired of their cat and mouse games. "I'll tell you. This expedition has been a disaster from the start. You've made wrong choices at every turn."

"What are you talking about?"

Min wasn't sure herself. "You let us get trapped. You might as well have led us straight into an ambush. And you didn't...well...there's other things, too."

Mac's face darkened. She'd struck a nerve. "Oh, I see what this is about," he fired back. "This is Minarra, Roger's only child, god's gift, pouting because she wasn't in charge. As if you could have done a damn thing different than I did."

That was the last straw. "No, asshole, that's where you're wrong," she challenged. "I don't wish I was in charge. I wish Daddy was, because he wouldn't have us chasing all over the fucking desert in the middle of the night like a bunch of chickens with our heads cut off. Jeezus, Mac, he'd have *your* head and you know it!"

Mac clenched his teeth. His voice went flat, level. "Yes...the great Roger Hunt...but he's not here. And I am. Pity for you, isn't it?" Grabbing something from the back of the jeep, he began pulling Minarra over the dune to the other side.

"Where are you taking me?" She demanded. "Are you insane?"

"I'm taking you for discipline," he informed her.

"But the rebels..."

"They can wait five minutes to kill us." He thrust her forward, facing him, a few feet away. They were in a small, sand-swept depression, hidden from the view of the others. On the far side, beyond the next ridge, lay the open, unguarded terrain. "Take down your pants, Min. Your underwear, too."

She watched as he laid his rifle down and took off his holster. He returned to her holding a leather strap, one of the all-purpose binding cords.

"What do you intend to do with that?" She demanded.

"I'm going to use it on you."

"You're going to whip me?" She laughed in disbelief. "I don't think so."

Minarra's heart quickened in dark anticipation. She did not long for pain, and yet the sheer audacity of the act, the wicked power and sinfulness of it was doing something to her loins — heating them and readying them.

"Apparently the spanking was not enough."

"You've spent too much time outside the States," she shook her head. "Things like this don't fly with us American women."

"As far as you know," he countered. "Now are you going to bare your ass like a good girl, or do you need help?"

"I'm not a girl, you cocksucker. I'm a woman."

"You're a subordinate. In need of correction."

"Is that all I am? Seems to me you did a lot more than subordinate me last night. But wait, I forgot, you're the king of mixed messages. Yesterday I'm good enough to marry, last night I was just a fuck buddy and now I'm what — some dog you want to work your frustrations out on?"

"You won't succeed in upsetting or insulting me, Minarra. Not by trivializing my emotions, not even by throwing your sainted father in my face."

God, he'd never looked sexier to her. Filled with adrenalin, testosterone pumping, fighting so hard to keep his true feelings under wraps. She wanted him to fuck her, right here and now, to take her to that other dimension, the realm of passion, where nothing mattered, not even life and death.

At the same time, she was furious with him, and confused and desperately wishing he could get her out of this place, to anywhere else.

"Emotions? How am I supposed to know what you're feeling?" She accused. "You hide everything."

"I think I have made my position clear enough." She could see the contradictions. The tension. The erection in his shorts, the clenched fists, the twitching lip. He wanted her, just like she wanted him. It was a primal thing, a hearkening back to ancient days, of caves and animal skins, when males protected and dominated their females. But something held him back. She'd felt it there, even yesterday when he'd proposed to her.

One way or the other she had to know.

"You want to beat me?" She challenged. "Is that the best thing you can think to do with me? Fine, I surrender—wreak havoc on my naked ass and then pass it along to Hassan and the others. They can whip me, too, and maybe even fuck me. How's that for a plan?"

"Don't be melodramatic. This is simple discipline. Between you and me."

"But it's not simple." Minarra was unbuttoning her khaki shirt, pulling it down over her shoulders. "You obviously have all these things to prove where I'm concerned. You need me to be your little harem girl, your desert slave—whatever. Well, here's your chance, baby. And why not? We're going to die, anyway."

"Get hold of yourself," he warned, as she shed the shirt and unhooked her bra.

Minarra sank to her knees, holding up her exposed breasts, pushing them together. "Use me," she said, her voice a husky, dark whisper. "Ravish me…now."

It was a call for her own subjugation, though Minarra was far from weak in the matter. When this was said and done, she'd pick up her gun again. Her own father had trained her to use it, and Mac knew that. No, this was about the sex, pure and simple. Sex in the desert, sex with danger, sex with role-playing.

"Get, up, Min."

"No." Defiantly she crawled to him, reaching for his crotch. He pushed her back onto the sand.

She went to him again, this time hugging his calves. "Take me," she hissed, biting into the back of his leg.

Mac cursed, grabbing her by the hair. He pulled her up, painfully, back to her knees. Her blood was pounding. He had her back bowed, enough to fully advertise the swell of her breasts. "You don't know what you are messing with, Min."

"Try me," she dared. Indeed, she was fearless. Under the skies of the ancients, the stars of the long ago merchants and vagabonds, she held nothing back. More than this, she sensed in her gut the pull of the city. Of Shera-Sa. It was calling. Just like Hassan had said was possible. She wondered if he knew the details…if he'd ever seen the gorgeous Komen-tah, or his mysterious priestess, those pure creatures of dark seduction.

Mac's face reflected her own torment — the craving of delicious pain, the feel of the moth, drawn to flame. Could he feel the power, too? Pulling down his zipper, he pulled his rock-hard erection from the opening.

"Don't say you didn't ask for this." He declared. "And I'll let you in on a little secret, too. Every time I've seen you lately I have wanted to do this — this and about a hundred other things to you. The desert agrees with you...you wench."

Mac guided her lips to the tip of his cock. His skin glowed in the moonlight. He smelled deep and rich, like a man should. The tip of his shaft was velvety smooth. Gladly she wrapped herself around him, working her way up the base. "Oh Min," he groaned. "That's so good. If only...if only. Oh Christ. You get my head so...scrambled."

It pleased her to be able to scramble him up for a change. Certainly, he'd done his share of that to her head. It pleased her even more at the moment, to be burying her fear, with all the seeming ease of burying the man's cock. Fumbling at her waistband, she tucked her hand in, edgewise. She was on a mission for her pussy and she would not be deterred.

He put his hands on her shoulders. "Don't want to come yet," he declared. "I wanna be inside — "

Mac went stiff. Ramrod straight. Like steel. The only motion was the pulsing of his warm cock. Something was wrong. The man had sensed something.

"Min," he whispered, his voice sharp as a Japanese blade. "We're not alone. Don't make any sudden movements. Disengage, quick and quiet as you can and crawl behind me."

Minarra knew this was not the time to argue. She could hear nothing herself, but she trusted him totally. Sliding her mouth off the end of his cock, she lowered herself to her hands and knees. Damn it. What a fool she'd been, playing sex games with him out here in the dunes.

"Now I want you to hand me the rifle," he said when she'd taken up her position behind his shins. "Nice and slow. Don't get up. Keep as low to the ground as you can."

Minarra lowered herself to her hip. She could barely see a hand in front of her face. Feeling in the sand, she found the rifle, grabbed it and handed it up to Mac. He took it nice and slow, keeping his arm at his side. With the weapon pointed to the ground, his finger on the trigger, he gave her his final orders.

"When I count to three," said Mac, his eyes still trained on the seemingly empty desert in front of them. "I want you to get up and run back to the jeep. As fast as you can. Alert Hassan, tell him my orders are for you to escape now. You are not to wait for me. Is that clear?"

Her poor heart felt like it was going to explode. She managed to grab her shirt, clutching it with a damp fist. "But...but Mac."

"Goddamn it, Min. Do it!"

"Yes..."

"One," he counted. "Two...and three."

Minarra bolted. Time went into slow motion. It was like one of those dreams where you try and run away, but you feel like your feet are stuck in place. Behind her she heard shouting, in Alcazaran. A shot rang out and then another. The crack of rifle fire. It never occurred to her that she could be shot. It was Mac she was scared for. She had to get him help. There was no way she'd let them go without him, even if she had to go back for him herself.

There was no need to sound any alarm. Hassan was already running toward her, several of the men with him.

"Mac needs help," she cried, pulling the shirt on to cover herself. "He's over the dune. "Fighting off some of the rebels!"

She left the part out about how they were all supposed to leave without him. It was insubordination to the max, but she'd be damned if she'd lose Mac out here. Not now. Not like this.

Hassan began shouting orders. Minarra ran to the back of the jeep, looking for her weapon. Seeing the mounted machine gun gave her a better idea. Starting up the vehicle, and turning on the headlights, she headed right for the dune. A little firepower would scare the bastards off...

She paused at the top of the dune. Looking down, in the beam of the lights, she could see Mac down, on his stomach. He was firing the pistol, attempting to pin down the enemy at several points. He had them at bay, a stalemate. Though it wasn't going to last long. He was vulnerable as hell from his position. Especially now that she was shining the lights down there.

Minarra hadn't a second to lose. She shut off the lights and listened. She could hear gunfire coming from the other way, requiring the men's attention. Climbing back over the seat, she grabbed the dual handle of the machine gun. She'd have to aim high, so as not to come anywhere near Mac. She'd never actually fired a gun this powerful, though her father had made sure to teach her how to use small arms as well as hand-held machine guns.

Spacing her feet solidly apart and pointing forward, she depressed the trigger. The gun crackled and boomed, spitting out death with fast muzzle flashes. All at once, the sky lit up. She'd managed to hit something, that was for sure. A fireball rose into the air and the rebels pulled back.

"Mac!" she called out, searching for him in the firelight.

By this time Hassan had caught up to her. Running down into the sand valley, he grabbed Mac and helped him to his feet. Mac put his arm around Hassan's shoulder. Minarra's heart seized. Mac had been shot.

Hassan helped him into the jeep, next to her. He'd been shot in the leg. Thank god it wasn't to a vital organ. Even so he was in pretty bad pain.

"Drink this, my friend," Hassan passed him a flask.

Mac took a deep swallow of whatever alcohol was inside. "I'll drive," he said, gritting his teeth.

"Like hell," said Minarra. "You're not fit to drive a golf cart. I'll drive, thank you very much."

"Hassan," he breathed, obviously weakened and woozy. "Tell this woman I am fit to take the wheel."

Hassan hesitated. She knew what a big deal it was in his culture to allow a woman to take preference over a man, especially a foreign woman. The mere fact that he was not instantly siding with Mac was all the encouragement she needed.

"I'll take the lead!" She announced. "You follow me, Hassan."

Hassan pursed his lips. "The rebels may yet be ahead of us," he pointed out. "Are you sure I or one of the others should not be in front?"

"There won't be any more rebels." Minarra startled herself with the authority in her voice. She had no idea how she knew this to be the case, but she did. From this point on, so long as they kept moving, there would be no further opposition. At least from the natural world.

Hassan studied her face in the moonlight. "You have the sight," he said. "I have watched you and thought it might be so, and now I know."

"The sight?"

"The sight of the priestess. There are some who connect to it. They are drawn here, from many places, to the old city, to Shera-Sa. It is a gift."

"A curse more like."

"Nonetheless, those who are called must follow it," said the big man soberly. "Just as we must follow you…"

Seconds later, they were on the road, once again under cover of darkness, speeding further into the desert, further from civilization. Mac was mumbling something about resting his eyes for a few minutes and then taking over, but it was clear he was hurt worse than he was letting on. Had he been hit more than once?

She considered stopping, to check on him, to let him rest. But the fact remained they might all die in that case. The only safety, for him, or any of them, lay in pushing on.

"You sure you're all right?" She asked.

"Yeah. Stop worrying about me and watch those potholes," he groused. "Women drivers…"

She gave him a light slap on the arm. "Watch your tongue," she chided, trying to keep her tone light and jovial.

It was her worst fear come true. Mac was dying.

Chapter Eight

Dawn found the little convoy utterly alone, surrounded by millions of cubic meters of sand. They were stopped at their rendezvous point, due to meet with a group of Bedouins Hassan had subcontracted to provide camel transport.

It was the end of the road. Literally. Mac was laid out on a section of canvas tent. Mahmoud, one of Hassan's men was kneeling beside him, attempting field surgery. He'd had some experience as a medic in the Alcazaran army, though he was hardly a doctor. Under the circumstances, however, it was the best they could do. Minarra was holding his hand, fighting back the tears. Cursing all the lost time, she would never forgive herself if he died now.

After all, she was responsible, too. For being too proud to pursue him. To demand he explain his sudden departure. In her heart she'd always wondered about the cause. Her own insecurities made her too timid to face rejection head-on, but what if it was something else?

Hassan said a morning prayer, asking his god to intervene. The wounds were indeed more serious than they'd first appeared. Mac had the bullet in his thigh, but there was also a second lodged in his shoulder. A third had grazed his temple. He'd been losing blood. There were twin dangers now. On the one hand, sepsis from the wound, and continued blood loss on the other. Surgery was costing more of his vital life fluid, but they couldn't afford to leave the bullets in.

"Don't you die on me," Minarra clasped his hand in hers. "You hear me, you stubborn son of a bitch?"

He looked up at her, focusing, hanging on her words. "Wouldn't...give you...the satisfaction," he groaned through gritted teeth.

Minarra laughed through watering eyes.

Hassan continued his incantations, beautiful, haunting words, ancient as the sand, proud as the rising sun and the blue sky. Minarra tried not to see the blood, the despair it represented. If the man died now, she would remember this always. A different kind of tragedy than losing her father. In the case of Roger Hunt, it had been an invisible killer. Microbes, a disease, an unbeatable foe, contracted on an expedition to the jungle.

They'd had to drag her from his body at the funeral home. She could not accept the reality that the lifeless gray skin could possibly belong to her father. It took the burial, seeing his body laid beside her mother, to finally convince her. Afterward she'd had the nightmares—chasing after him in the jungle, trying to protect him from all manner of deadly creatures, panthers and creeping vines, hissing snakes and biting insects.

She wouldn't, couldn't lose another man in her life. So many things she'd never asked her father. She'd never known what made him tick. Why he was as sullen as he'd been, why quiet and angry, why obsessed. And why, never, ever, had he been able to say he loved her. A million other things—powerful protective things, a whole wall of security in his words—but never the three she wanted most. I love you.

No wonder she couldn't deal well when Mac said them.

No wonder...

Damn it, she couldn't go there. She had to get him through this. The blood. It was real. She couldn't look away. She couldn't deny it. She had to go into the fire, stand with him.

But with the blood...came terror.

She blinked, trying to force it from her eyes. Something gripping her. She sought to focus only on Mahmoud's tiny knife, making its precise incision. The ugly gray slug underneath. It was too hard to fight though...it was the shower all over again. Red, trickling fluid.

The river turned to blood. Like the Nile in the Bible.

Minarra felt faint. The voices around her were hollow.

"She's exhausted," said Hassan. "Lay her down."

She tried to shake her head no. *Don't separate us...*

* * * * *

All at once, her world was swallowed in darkness. She feared she was drowning again, but as she breathed, new life flooded her lungs. A flash of light, and she was standing before an altar, a black marble disc, floating midair. On either side, two pure gold columns. A ring of gems hung in the air, arrayed like the setting of a diamond ring. Minarra looked about. She was outside, standing on what appeared to be a small platform. On closer examination, she saw it was the top of a structure, the small, flat roof of a pyramid. One among many pyramids. A city of them. There were spires, too, and domes, incredible architecture on all sides. Banners hung from some of the spires, colored in brilliant golds and purples.

There were statues too, hundreds of feet high, flanking colored stone streets. Eagles merged with lions, a serpent with four heads and the flanks of a bear. A whole array of mythical creatures, some known to her and some brand-new.

She drew a deep, sharp breath as she realized the implications. She was seeing Shera-Sa. She was there...in it, as it was. Or was it merely more of her own dream projections?

"You ask the correct questions, my dear," said a voice, melodic and exquisitely female.

Minarra turned back to the altar, though the voice was everywhere, even in her head.

"I have waited long to speak with you," said the beautiful, dark-haired woman, arrayed as an Egyptian priestess. "I am she who shares your name. I am Minar-ra, Intercessor of the People."

Minarra licked her lips. She'd never seen a creature so dazzling. Her blue gown, light and pleated silk, glowed. Her skin was the color of mocha, her shoulders graceful and smooth below the delicate, thin straps of her costume. A thin golden cord circled her waist, accentuating her hips and perfect breasts. On closer examination, she saw the cord was actually a small snake, with green eyes and a red tongue.

The snake looked at Minarra and hissed.

The priestess touched the head of it, and said a word to quiet it. The gesture came too late to dispel Minarra's sense of danger. This priestess was not to be trusted.

"You cannot but trust me," Minar-ra read her mind again. "Our thoughts are one. I've known you from your birth. I've cultivated you. Once, a long time ago, I knew your father, too."

Minarra shook her head. "I am not with you. I have my own life."

Mac.

"Yes..." Minar-ra attached herself to this at once. "The Mummy Hunter. He has amused us for some time."

A surge of protectiveness went through her, combined with sheer rage. She'd been running long enough. From her own fears. From her past, and lately from a group of gun toting bullies who'd shot the one man who'd ever helped her to be a woman.

"If you do anything to hurt Mac," swore Minarra, "I will kill you."

Minar-ra smiled. It was not a smile of kindness. Not a living smile at all. "You love him, don't you?"

The words were filled with scorn, accusation.

"You're in my head," spat Minarra. "Answer your own questions."

"You should watch your tongue, my little daughter. Especially given that I am the only one who can save your precious Mummy Hunter."

"What are you talking about? Save him?"

She raised her arm, her long slender fingers tipped with blood-red nails. "Life flows through these fingers. And death."

"You aren't a goddess," Minarra defied. "I don't even think you exist at all."

"That's where you're wrong. Or will be shortly."

She recognized Komen-tah's voice, his arrogant tone, at once. The skin on the back of her neck crawled as he strode past, taking up his place at the altar beside the priestess.

"My lord." The priestess melted, putting her lips to his.

Komen-tah, wearing nothing but a loincloth of black leather and black leather armbands, ran his hand up and down the side of her body. He was a specimen of sheer physical delight. Ribbed abdomen, perfectly sculpted pectorals, and deliciously shaped ass. He was also, she was quite sure, a force of sheer malevolence. Bending his muscular, bull neck, he whispered a word in the woman's ear.

Minarra heard it clear enough.

"Adoration."

The lovely priestess fell to her knees, kissing Komen-tah's crotch.

"She worships me, now," explained the prince. "I am the only god in Shera-Sa. You will worship me, too."

"I'd tell you to go to hell," said Minarra. "But they've probably already sent you back."

Komen-tah laughed. "You have spirit. I like that. Perhaps I will make you one of my personal slaves when I conquer the earth."

"You and what army?"

Minarra regretted her choice of words. She'd already gotten a hint of that army, in one of her earlier visions.

Growling, the prince pushed aside his loincloth, took his priestess by the hair and shoved her head onto his erect, mammoth cock. Nearly a foot long, she absorbed it in submissive delight. "You wish to see my power? Very well."

Taking the snake belt from Minar-ra, he snapped it straight. At once it turned into a staff, long and pointed, tipped in emeralds. This in turn, he pointed to the sky. Thunder cracked and the blue heavens opened to reveal a swirl of red, bleeding clouds. A host of chariots emerged, with black-armored warriors. After this, men on horseback, their faces covered with silver masks. They held the glowing swords she'd seen earlier. Behind them, foot soldiers, ancient in bearing, but holding odd energy weapons, like lassos that at once protected them and allowed them to strike out at the enemy.

She saw war now, war upon war as one by one the nations of the earth fell to this strange new power. A power Komen-tah had found in his earthly life, but had somehow been prevented from using. It had taken the sinking of his entire city, but the black magic of Shera-Sa had never overwhelmed the earth.

"This is my kingdom...my destiny," he cried.

Minarra saw the millions, the billions of people, on their knees to this madman—surrendering submitting. It was no wonder the gods had destroyed him.

"I am...the only god," he shouted. His fine buttocks were pumping furiously. His eyes were rolling in his head. Minar-ra was swallowing his come, gulping it down. When he'd subsided he pushed her away. She put her head to the ground before rising once more to her knees.

"Don't defy me," warned Komen-tah pointing his finger at Minarra. "You will obey and you will obey now. Submit your mind to me, let me in!"

"I can save your lover," said Minar-ra, reiterating her own softer appeal for Minarra's alliance.

Two things occurred to Minarra simultaneously. First, they needed her for some reason. If they could conquer the world already, they would have. They'd been after her for some time, luring her with dreams, trying to scare and bully her. What power exactly did she have that they needed her to surrender?

Secondly, it dawned on her that Minar-ra could not read all her thoughts. She was blind to one thing at least. Love. It was alien to her. Foreign to both of them. Love would be the shield she'd wrap around her secret thoughts, her plan.

She loved Seth Macallister. And that would save them both.

Minar-ra looked at her curiously, head cocked.

"What is it?" Demanded Komen-tah of his sexual surrogate.

"She is…holding back."

Komen-tah stepped toward Minarra. "You have not learned…"

Minarra stepped backward to the edge. "Stop where you are, or I will jump."

"You would never kill yourself."

"To prevent your mad scheme?" She challenged. "I'd do it in a heartbeat."

Komen-tah frowned, uncertain.

"My Lord," said the priestess, "let me intervene…let me serve."

"Very well, but be quick about it."

"Minarra," said Minar-ra, with her mind-soaking voice. "Cooperate with us and I will spare the life of your Mummy Hunter. I will see to it he is returned safely home."

Minarra focused on her deep feelings. How she'd felt about Mac from the moment she had laid eyes on him. Behind this cloak, she reasoned it out. Gaining protection for him now would mean nothing if these two gained control of the whole earth. Neither Mac nor anyone else would be safe, ever again. Still, she must appear to go along until she could see a way to defeat them.

"How do I know you'll keep your end of the bargain?" She asked, making sure not to agree too easily.

"You have my word," said Komen-tah. "As a god."

"Forgive me if I'm skeptical," she said dryly.

"I will share my sight with you," suggested Minar-ra. "You will be allowed to watch as he is preserved.

That had possibilities. If Minarra could get into the priestess's mind as the priestess was in hers. "That might work," said Minarra. "But I need to know what you want from me."

"Take a guess," Komen-tah grinned. He was holding his cock, fully erect again, as if nothing had happened.

"You must take My Lord's semen, and join us."

So that was it. He needed to join forces with a living being…he needed her soul, or whatever was inside her that gave her the spark of life. For all their bravado, these two clowns were still stuck in the land of the shadows. They were powerless, like any other ghosts.

"Will you be…gentle?" Asked Minarra, feigning the part of awestruck maiden. "You are so…virile."

For all his supposed omniscience and omnipotence, Komen-tah proved as easily deceived by his own ego as any other male. "This is true...and I will not lie—no mortal female can be fully prepared. But if you submit, utterly, if you worship me, I shall be merciful as your god."

"Thank you...My Lord...it's...it's been on my mind, you know? I've fought my desires, so long..."

"All females must yield eventually. Minar-ra did also. She resisted once. Now she has learned."

Minarra glanced at her name's sake. Was there an ounce of fight left in the ghost priestess? Could she turn these two against each other?

"I-I'm scared," said Minarra, seeking to make herself appear as harmless as possible.

"Fear is good. Remove your clothing," he ordered. "On your back. Spread your legs in preparation."

"And Mac?" She reminded.

"I shall tend to him now...behold. Minar-ra, make it so."

Minar-ra stood at her Lord's command, raising her arms. At once the scene went dark. Winds swirled about them and as the merely human Minarra clenched her eyes tightly she could hear the voices, of Hassan and the others. His prayer, and the talk of the medic, mingling, with Mac's low groans.

* * * * *

Opening her eyes again, she was there. She sat up on the bedroll they'd laid her on. Clambering to her feet, she ran to Mac's side.

Mahmoud drew a breath. Light glinted off the end of his blade. "My hand," he cried. "It is possessed."

Mahmoud shook his head as the blade began to dance at his fingertips. "I…this isn't me," he insisted as the scalpel did its work.

In seconds, the bullet popped out. "Give me some gauze," said Minarra, attempting to keep him on track. "Get the one in his shoulder."

"But…the blood."

Minarra slapped down the gauze. Instinctively she knew the wound would be instantly healed now, and the blood replaced. Sure enough, a second later she took the material off and found nothing, not even a scratch.

It was the same with the shoulder. In a matter of minutes, the man had been healed of two serious wounds.

"Min?" He sat up, groggy, but very much alive. "What the hell happened? We were out in the dunes…"

She blushed, thinking what they'd been doing out there. "Yeah, we were."

"Thank god," he pulled her into his arms. "You're safe."

Her heart went to her throat. This felt so good. If only it could be permanent. If only she hadn't made that bargain. Maybe they'd forget. Maybe that part was all a dream…

* * * * *

Mac held onto Minarra for all he was worth. She had saved his life. He didn't know how, but he was sure it was her.

"It's a miracle," Mahmoud was crying.

Hassan was weeping, a gesture of uncharacteristically deep emotion for a man like him. Several of the others were on their knees in prayer to various gods of their religions.

"Min...oh, Minarra, I love you," he gasped.

Minarra went limp in his arms. He called her name again. She did not respond. Instinctively, he knew where she was. Sucked into that dream world of hers—whatever it was that was sucking her in from Shera-Sa. "Hassan," he called out. "Come here quickly."

Hassan helped him to lay her back down. He knelt on one knee and examined her pupils. Frowning, he took her pulse. Twice he nodded, gravely.

"What is it?" demanded Mac. "Tell me already."

"She has the sight," he explained. "And now she is deep in trance."

Mac listened as Hassan told him of the old legends of the priestess Minar-ra, controlling the minds of certain persons, drawing them into the desert. He'd heard much of this before, from Roger. Roger had taken more and more to the occult in his later years. Mac had always wondered how healthy that was, especially for Min. It was bad enough that Roger had named her for that ancient priestess in the first place.

That kind of thing could haunt a person, even swallow them whole.

A chill grabbed Mac's spine. What if she had been swallowed? What if her mind was trapped somewhere now? He had to find some way to bring her out. "Hassan—I need to be put in that trance, too."

He shook his head. "That, my friend, I cannot do."

"But I can." This from Mahmoud, his face strangely luminescent, his voice oddly calm.

"No." Hassan spoke sharply. "It is too dangerous."

"You can really do it?" Mac grabbed Mahmoud's upper arms, ignoring Hassan.

He nodded. "Something passed through me, something…used me… It came down a pathway. I felt Minarra's presence go down that way. I…you could follow it. If your heart is in tune with hers."

"Why should I believe any of this?" said Mac.

"You shouldn't," Hassan said quickly.

"I was apprentice to a shaman," Mahmoud defended his credentials. "Before the army. "I acquired some sensitivity. But Hassan is correct. There is no proof one way or the other."

"There's only one way to find out," Mac said.

"But there is a risk," said Hassan. "You have not told him that, Mahmoud."

Mahmoud nodded. "It is true. If you follow the woman and are not bonded to her, the others will seize you."

"The priestess," said Mahmoud. "And the prince. Her lover. They seek to reawaken. The legend says they must co-habit with a human soul, a sympathetic energy source. This will allow them re-birth in flesh, with all the powers they once held."

"Minarra is the one I love," he said simply. "I am prepared to die for her."

"But she must accept you, my friend," warned Hassan. "If she has any negative feelings toward you…she will not be able to hold you. Your soul will be torn to shreds. And hers."

Mac put his hand on the man's shoulder. "And if I do nothing…she will die anyway. And all of us besides."

Hassan nodded. "I accept your logic."

"Good. Mahmoud, tell me what I need to do."

"Nothing," said Mahmoud, putting his hand on Mac's forehead. "Other than close your eyes. And take a deep breath."

"I don't have to click my heels three times?"

"Eh?" Mahmoud missed the *Wizard of Oz* reference.

"Never mind," Mac shook his head, taking the requisite breath.

"Concentrate," whispered Mahmoud as Mac closed his eyes. "And concentrate on Minarra. Think of what you feel for her…your desire to be with her."

A vision of her flashed in his mind, the way she'd been when he'd first laid eyes on her. Feisty, challenging, sexy as hell, without the least awareness of her power over men. That had been Roger's doing, keeping her sheltered like that from her sexuality.

Mac imagined his first conversation with Minarra. The heated debate over the age of the Sphinx, and whether it could have originated with a civilization prior to the Egyptians.

She'd been so animated, her pupils dilated, those ruby lips so very serious. "So what do you think?" She'd asked when she'd laid out her thesis.

"I think I'd like to kiss you," he'd replied.

From there it was a blur, from the first taste of her all the way to now. He registered in his life two realities. Her presence, which was light, and her absence, which was dark.

"Yes," Mahmoud said, reading his mind. "This is the path to follow…she is ahead of you. Keep concentrating."

Mac focused himself, even more tightly, on an image of Minarra's face. Those eyes of hers, the deepest blue he'd ever seen. The dimples, the tiny lines by her mouth, at once playful and guarded. The dual, paradoxical nature of her expressions, hopeful and tragic. Her chin, so delicate, yet noble. Always, though, it was back to the eyes. That is where a man lost himself.

Mac allowed himself to drift into them. Another set of eyes within eyes, closed, and he was at a deeper place. His own heartbeat was loud and clear.

"Find your body now," said Mahmoud. "A body within your body…gravity… weight."

Mac hung in the air of nothingness, lost in the blue eyes, and then, suddenly, he felt himself harden like a stone. The bottom dropped from beneath him. He was plunging, down into the depths of a bottomless black hole. He tried to scream but nothing came out. He was sure he would keep on falling forever, but incredibly, he impacted on a soft, spongy surface. He bounced and was absorbed.

The material he was on was wet and sticky. He struggled to free his limbs. It was like being a fly stuck on a piece of flypaper. The harder he tried, the more entangled he felt.

"I can't go on," he breathed, stuck flat on his back.

"You must," Mahmoud spoke to his mind. "What you seek lies straight ahead."

He would do it for Minarra. He would find the energy. Making a phenomenal effort, he tore himself free and rose to his feet. The next thing he knew, he was running down a dark corridor. There was a bright yellow light at the end of it.

What he sought was straight ahead.

He would reach it, but he had no clue if he would be prepared.

* * * * *

Minarra stood at the back of the temple, facing the twin-columned flames and the sacred consummation bed. She was naked, her body adorned in golden chains. Shackles upon her ankles and wrists, the slender links crisscrossing her breasts and looping about her belly. Her hair was atop her head, spun with gold and set with diamonds, emeralds and topaz. On either side of her, prostrate, were rows of slave girls, in various colored silks.

Her bare feet rested upon a runner of dyed fiber, so soft that it might well have been silk. Ahead of her, at the end of the runner, flanking the bed, six hooded, castrated priests stood ready to chain her down for Prince Komen-tah. It was her duty to walk the aisle, between the rows of slaves, in preparation for making of herself a naked offering.

Komen-tah was being prepared by Minar-ra, who was rubbing oil all over his rock-hard body. She did not leave out his cock, which was larger and more erect than she recalled previously. In many ways, it was like being in a trance. Her real body was not even here and yet she was acutely aware that what was going on, reflected the deeper reality of her being and that of the world as well.

So far she'd concocted nothing by way of a plot to defeat the prince. Behind the protective wall of her love for

Mac, she could summon only a desire to have him here. A foolish, wishful thought that did nothing but divert her energy from real strategizing. She was so tired, though. She'd been fighting this battle for so long, alone. Truly, she did not know if she had much more left in her. The one thing she'd rallied herself for was to save Mac. The rest of it, even her own life, just didn't seem that important.

If Komen-tah wanted her soul so badly, perhaps she should just give it to him. It was in this listless mood that Minarra found herself as the masked eunuchs chained her down. They secured her spread-eagle, one limb at each corner of the ornate, hand-carved bed.

There were furs atop it, symbols of Komen-tah's prowess, presumably. The furs were luxurious, almost pleasant where they tickled her exposed flesh. Her exposed pussy responded with tingling heat. Much as she loathed the touch of the prince, she could not help the physical stimulation the position was providing.

If only this could be Mac coming for her…

"You look lovely, my dear," cooed Komen-tah. "I am so glad you have agreed to take the intelligent course and serve me."

"Like you said, Prince. No one defies you and gets away with it."

He continued to stroke himself, his eyes lit with a dark heat as he stood over her. "Indeed, my priestess. Indeed."

Damn it. She should be thinking of something by now. Some way to turn this all around, to turn these two against each other, to put it all to her own advantage…

She was so freaking useless. An emotional woman. Like her mother. *No wonder Daddy was never satisfied.*

Komen-tah began to laugh. "Poor miserable little Minarra. Never makes anyone happy."

Fuck. Now they were both reading her mind.

"How would you like to join him?" Asked Komen-tah taking a hooked knife from the priestess. "In the afterlife. You can lament to each other for all eternity."

Minarra tensed in her bonds. "You said this was a sexual ritual."

"You think I need only a female opening to come in?" He scorned. "Do you think that is all your sacrifice will entail? No, little one. You will give me blood as well. Every ounce of it. Enough to saturate the city, to give it back its life."

She thought of the dreams, of the floods, of the rivers of blood. "Komen-tah, don't do this."

"I do as I will." He raised the knife overhead, and then lowered it smoothly onto his own arm. He made a single sweep, slicing across his biceps. A line of red appeared. Lifting his head to the vaulted, bricked ceiling of the mammoth chamber, he began to laugh.

The sound chilled Minarra to the bone. She felt the seconds ticking, her life draining away. She had but one regret. Not being able to see Mac ever again. To touch him or to kiss him. Or even to fight with him.

Damn, this was going to be harder than she thought…this dying business. Especially with that sense in her mind that Mac was so close to her. Why did her mind have to play such cruel tricks, now of all times.

Or was it a trick? She focused her internal eyes, trying to see. Could it be he was out there, trying to reach her? Tentatively she sent out feelers. Her mind moved into quick, cold survival mode. If he was there, there was not only a reason, but also a chance to live. A plan formed in her mind, based upon the possibilities latent in the temple. There were weapons on the wall, shields and swords. It was a long shot, but not impossible.

After all, this place that was Komen-tah's sanctuary, could yet be his tomb.

* * * * *

Mac heard her calling out. Minarra was at the end of the tunnel, somewhere in the golden light. If only it weren't so damned difficult to get there. It felt like he'd run a mile, but he was no closer. It could go on forever at that rate.

What he needed was to try and call back to her, to set up a link. Opening his mind, he threw his thoughts, like a beacon in her direction. At first there was nothing. Then, very faintly, he caught a wisp. The sound of her breathing. The smell of her perfume. The trill of her voice, a rising sound. A whisper at first, beckoning, and then, more plaintive. He had to clear the blockage in his mind, to hear. He had to blast free his thought processes, quickening them to lightning.

There, he had it. Like an internal code, they flashed back and forth. He was able to read her situation—what was going on in the room she was in, and what he needed to do when he got there.

There's a spear on the wall, to the left when you enter. You must grab it, and the sword beside it.

Mac found them and took them down at once, not pausing to survey the rest of his surroundings. He was glad he did because the minute he yanked it off the wall

Prisoner of Shera-Sa

there were a hundred shrieking women all pointing at him. They were wearing silk—harem girls.

"Seize him," called a woman from the front of the chamber.

A half-dozen masked men, priests from the look of them, came charging toward him at once.

They are eunuchs, came the voice of Minarra. *They'll flee at the wave of the sword. The one you have to kill is the big dude with the knife.*

Mac grumbled his telepathic reply. *Why is it always the big dudes with knives you have to kill? Why can't it ever be the little guys who piss their pants at the sight of you?*

"Who dares intrude on the sacred ritual?" Roared the ugly dude with the knife. "Kill him," he pointed.

The eunuchs, as predicted, ran after a few passes of Mac's sword in the air.

"Traitors," roared the big man, who looked like one of those pro wrestlers. "I will kill you all for this."

The interesting thing was, Mac had actually nicked one of the eunuchs, or at least he'd passed his sword through what should have been a part of him only to find himself slicing thin air.

They're not alive, Mac thought to Minarra. *That will make killing any of them a little more difficult. Oh, by the way, thanks for saving my life. I assume that was you?*

It was. Though I shouldn't have bothered, after the horrid way you treated me in the desert.

You pick a fine time to start a fight.

I chat when I'm nervous. I can't help it.

In that case, chat to your big friend. See if you can distract him.

"Komen-tah," Minarra spoke aloud. "I need you…come and make love to me…you know I have pledged myself to you."

"I told you," he said, already moving toward Mac. "I want your blood, not your sex."

"Then take my blood…now…do not risk being killed. This man is a great fighter," pleaded Minarra.

The big man bought the reverse psychology. They always did, even the five-thousand-year-old-ghost ones. The only question was how exactly could Mac defeat him, even if he could get in a clean shot?

You have to aim for the heart.

He hasn't any, Min… Mac beamed back to her mind.

Trust me, Mac, when it's time…he will.

The ancient prince was on him now, so there really wasn't time for further debate. Growling, he slashed full force, to and fro, attempting to rip him immediately to shreds. Mac held him off with the spear, avoiding instant death. The question was, how long could he hold out against a man, a force, this strong?

At least he'd die in sight of Minarra, defending her. From where he stood, there was nothing else in life that mattered.

* * * * *

Minarra hadn't much time. Komen-tah would slice Mac to ribbons unless she got to him first. There was, however, the little problem of the chains. The only one to help her was Minar-ra. At first look, the priestess would seem the least likely candidate to help her. On the other

Prisoner of Shera-Sa

hand, she was also his first victim, the one he'd first deceived with his lies about being a god.

Could it be she was tired of him? That she might be made to switch sides? With just a little sisterly influence?

Minar-ra was standing by, uncertain of what she should do. Minarra touched her mind, using their two-way link. At once the thoughts buzzed back and forth. The priestess wanted to shut her down, but Minarra kept fighting back, beaming her own perceptions of Komen-tah over and over. Let her see this joker for who he really was.

Minar-ra did not want to hear. "Silence!" she commanded aloud, threatening Minarra with a knife of her own.

The chained Minarra had no defense but to convince her. "Why do you fear my words? If they are not true? Or could it be you have doubts?"

"Komen-tah awakened me," she leaned over putting the blade to Minarra's throat. "He saved me from oblivion. Just as once before, in our earthly lives, he saved me from ignorance. There is no god but him."

"Then why does he need me, Minar-ra? Why can he not make his will happen alone? Unless he is consorting in the black arts—just another evil-hearted magician."

"I will kill you," she swore.

"Go ahead. But you know the truth. Your precious Komen-tah is a liar. He does not love you. He wants me. Read my memories. The dreams he placed there. He has lust for me and every other woman. He will betray you, when he is done using you."

Minar-ra's mind absorbed the dreams, the impressions. Doubt came bubbling to the surface at once. Her armor was cracking.

Immediately, Komen-tah turned to see what was going on. "Minar-ra...you are not concentrating...I am not receiving the flow."

Min's assumption was correct. Minar-ra was channeling for him, filtering some form of energy latent in the old city's ruins. She was keeping this all going, this entire energy and matter flux. And their generated beings, too, in this place of stasis. Without Minar-ra's function as a transfer agent, Komen-tah's power would whither. She'd been right in her advice to him—he should have absorbed her soul before facing Mac. Now he would have to do it on his own.

"Komen-tah, you lied to me!"

"Minar-ra, stop prattling woman, I command you, restore my power!"

Minar-ra dropped the knife and backed to the altar. It was as if a cloud had been lifted from her face. "What have we been doing?" She touched her cheeks. "We have been...committing sacrilege...again."

"It isn't so!" Cried Komen-tah. "Get hold of yourself!"

Mac was pushing the prince backward, parrying and thrusting. Twice he jabbed him in the ribs. Komen-tah was bleeding real blood—he was losing his energy form and taking on a physical one.

"*You* get hold of yourself," Mac growled, offering a deep thrust.

Komen-tah cried out, grabbing his midsection. The spear was halfway through him. His face and legs began to shimmer, like they might blink out, but out of his belly was pouring liquid—water, mixed with blood.

The flood.

"Mac," Minarra called out. "We have to get out of here."

Mac ran to her, passing Minar-ra as he did. The priestess knelt beside the fallen Prince Komen-tah, weeping. "I am sorry," she sobbed over and over.

He reached up too, calling her his one true love.

The waters were already filling the chamber, an inch deep. Mac reached Minarra and went to work on the chains. Using the priestess's knife, he opened the locks, freeing her wrists and ankles. Lifting her, he cradled her, like a newborn.

"We haven't much time," said Min. "We need to take the front way, through the curtain."

"Are you sure?" asked Mac.

"It's on the map," she said, surer than she had been of anything in her life. "It's been in my dreams, too. Now hurry, please."

The waters were knee-deep as they reached the sacred curtain. Pulling it aside, Mac exposed a stone wall, intricately carved.

"Let me," said Min.

He let her run her fingers through the grooves, forming an organized pattern. It was an activation signal, to release the wall's mechanism. Part of the mysterious technology of Shera-Sa. The real one that had existed in the place of this ghost domain.

"Come on," she hissed, forced to repeat the pattern a second time.

The waters were up to Mac's waist now, blood red, rising fast. He stood silent, patiently waiting for her to finish the job. He didn't doubt her. She was grateful for that. It meant the world to her.

At last the wall split apart, a jagged but regular line opening between two sliding halves. An opening was created in the ten-foot-high wall, wide enough for several men to fit through. Mac leaped through, Min still in his arms. The door shut behind them instantaneously.

"What took you so long?" Grumbled an old, all too familiar voice.

Minarra gasped. She was staring at a throne of gold, upon which sat the living image of her father. "Daddy?"

"Who else would it be, young lady?" As always, his patience was short for ignorant questions. "Seth, put her down, boy, let her come to me."

Seth, as stunned as she was, let Minarra's feet touch smoothly on the polished floor.

Minarra walked, scarcely aware of her feet. *This is still a dream*, she told herself.

"Hurry," he said. "There isn't much time. This is not a stable dimension."

"Daddy?" She touched his face. "Are you real?"

"I trained you better than that, Minarra. What are the only questions worth asking?"

"Those with provable, empirical answers," she recited, tugging playfully at his pointed beard.

"Correct," he shooed her off with a scowl. "Whether or not I 'exist' only as a figment of your imagination or as some mysterious poltergeist is irrelevant, and cannot be proven. The relevant matter, the interesting matter is whether I have anything to say that might impact your understanding of the world and your place in it."

"And do you?" She smiled, recalling at once how charming and exasperating the man could be.

"I have one thing to say—and you will have the rest of your days to contemplate whether or not you knew this in your heart and were therefore capable of dreaming it, and me, up. Seth did not leave you of his own accord. I forced his hand."

Min's heart skipped a beat. Had she suspected as much? "You, Daddy?"

"I didn't want you with someone like him... Someone like me. I thought you ought to do better."

"But Daddy. You were the man I admired most."

"You were biased, terribly so, by your upbringing. I ought to have raised you to hate me. It would have done you a great service."

She laughed at that. "If only you could hear yourself sometimes. But, Daddy, it doesn't matter. You couldn't have forced Seth to do anything. He was a grown man."

"It's true." Mac stepped forward. "Sir, I will not allow you to take that responsibility. You acted in good faith. I, in following your will, however, made a terrible mistake."

"We all make mistakes. Our lives are built on them. What is a non-mistake," expounded Roger, "but the substance of a life unlived, a hand unplayed. Shera-Sa was my mistake...it was the hand I played. But the same man who hunted a dead city his whole life also birthed you, Minarra..."

"And loved my mother..."

"You want me to forgive myself?" He smiled.

"I want us all to forgive," said Minarra.

Roger nodded approvingly. "I think you have your answer, then, as to the meaning of seeing me again."

"You know there's more." Minarra's eyes filled with tears. Outside, around them, she could hear the roar of the water. The city was flooding. The dream city of Shera-Sa. These walls would hold, but not for long. "Something else I want to hear."

"I know that," nodded Roger. "And I'll say what you want. But will that really make you happy?"

Minarra blinked, confused. More than anything she'd wanted to know her father loved her, and here, it seemed was the perfect chance to obtain her proof. But to do so now, by whatever means this was, supernatural or otherwise, felt like a cheat. The only true resolution lay in her heart. For the image of Roger Hunt could say anything at all, but it was up to her to believe.

"No," she decided. "That will not make me happy."

"What then?"

"This." She reached her hand out for Mac. He came forward and took it, grasping her fingers tightly. "Daddy," she presented herself, side by side with the man she loved. "I know you always meant well. I know your heart. And here, in the person of this man, is my heart."

Roger offered a broad smile. "You two had best be on your way," he chastised. "I won't be responsible if you drown like a pair of lovesick rats."

"Rats don't fall in love," Minarra pointed out.

"That's because they are too smart for it," he quipped.

Minarra gave him a kiss on the cheek. Mac gave him a hug. *Daddy loved them both.* And the only one who could prove that was her, looking at him, just as she remembered him. Like this. Full of spit and vinegar and cockeyed wisdom.

"Goodbye, Daddy. See you in the afterlife?"

He gave a wink. "I told you. No cheating the system. You'll have to die and find out like everyone else."

It was at that point the walls crashed in and the water came rushing over their heads.

* * * * *

Mac and Minarra came to, back in the desert. Mac was right where he'd been all along, with Mahmoud's hand on his forehead. Minarra was lying on the bedroll. Only seconds had passed and nothing at all seemed to have changed. Except their feelings for one another, born of the harrowing, life and death experience they'd just been through.

Without a word, they took their places in each other's arms. Neither had any intention of letting the other go. Ever again.

"Am I to assume the situation has resolved itself?" Asked Hassan.

"She's safe now," said Mac. "Nothing out there will hurt her anymore."

"And the city?"

"Shera-Sa is gone," Minarra spoke up. "It has been for five thousand years."

Hassan smiled knowingly. "You no longer seek it, then?"

"No. I found what I was looking for," she hugged Mac. "Or should I say, it found me."

"So the expedition is called off?" Mahmoud wondered.

Mac was about to speak, but he deferred to Minarra. "You need to ask our expedition leader. Our rightful leader."

"Co-leader," she grinned, hand on his chest. "And as far as my vote goes, I say we go back home."

"Ditto for me," said Mac.

A cheer went up from the men.

"There is the small problem of making it back past the rebels. And from there, gaining safe passage through Porto Sayeed," pointed out Hassan.

"That may not be a problem after all," said Mahmoud. "Look."

All eyes turned to the sky. There were helicopters, a large force of them. They bore military markings, but not those of the Alcazaran army.

Minarra was the first to recognize. "They're ours," she said excitedly. "They're Americans."

A pair of military helicopters set down in the nearby sand. A captain explained the situation. The security situation had degenerated and terrorists were threatening vital interests. US troops had been called in to restore order.

"We have room for all of you," the officer said. "Minus your gear."

"That," Hassan said, "we will happily surrender."

Mac caught up to Minarra, just as she was about to board one of the copters. "You forgot the map," he said.

She looked at the attaché case. "Leave it here," she decided. "With the rest of the relics."

Mac tossed it and jumped aboard after her. They sat side by side, holding hands all the way back to the capital. They had one thing on their minds, and it had nothing to do with ghosts or lost cities.

*****

Minarra lay reclined in the bed, shortly before midnight. The ceiling fan was clacking louder than ever in their old suite, but it was one of the sweetest sounds she'd ever heard. So was the sound of Mac in the bathroom, whistling as he shaved his face in readiness for a night of passion. She herself was freshly bathed and perfumed, dressed in a light silk robe, nothing underneath.

What a lucky, romantic break that they'd been able to stay on in the city overnight. The rebels, it seemed, had fled back into the dunes, no longer a threat to the government. This meant they could consummate their love for each other in a familiar setting. Really, they'd been in love all along, though they hadn't been willing to admit it, at least not to each other — at the same time.

It seemed almost comical now, the way they'd let these years slip by. Maybe it was good, though, because they were both more mature now, ready for a commitment.

Mac emerged wearing nothing but a towel. With his splendid, squeaky-clean body, she could almost imagine him as that ancient prince. But Mac was better looking in her opinion, warmer in his features. Plus, he was her man and that made her justifiably biased. Of all men on the planet, he was the only one who'd ever been able to make her wet with just a look.

Even now, she was ready. Could he smell her fragrance? The soft scent of her womanhood mixed with the perfume?

"You're so beautiful," he said, his eyes moist with need.

Min had never seen a sight so beautiful herself. "Mac," she whispered, as he crawled into bed on top of her. "I love you."

"I love you too," he murmured. "My little priestess."

She sighed happily as his hand undid the sash of her robe. Everything was possible, every form of loving between them, endless varieties, for the rest of their lives. For now, she wanted him to sink between her parted thighs.

"No one else has ever been here, you know. I meant it when I told you that."

He shuddered at the sensation, not to mention the comment. "I wouldn't care if they had," he teased her. "But I would be lying if I said my male ego wasn't gratified just a little."

"Hmmph. Typical male double standard. You've had other women and that's not supposed to bother me..."

"I've slept with others," he acknowledged. "But I tried to make every one of them into you."

She clung to him, exhaling with his sweet confession. "You're so wonderful, Mac. Tell me I'll never live without you again."

"Don't ask questions," he teased, "which have no empirical answers."

She grabbed his taut buttock pinching it. "Does that feel empirical enough for you?"

"Yes," he growled, thrusting hard and fast. "It does."

There was no more talking after that. Only loving, the interplay of bodies, the trading of desires, the ultimate consummation—hand in glove, his body in hers, her spirit in his. Their sexes joined, their hearts were one.

A truth written in stone. A reality that would outlast any monument, any city and any ruler.

Enjoy this excerpt from
Dance of Submission
© Copyright Reese Gabriel, 2004

All Rights Reserved, Ellora's Cave Publishing, Inc.

He was pointing straight at her.

The most beautiful man Persephone had ever seen. Half-Polynesian, half-Anglo, utterly naked save for a strip of white cloth tied round his firm waist. With or without the pair of mai tais, she'd have been resilient as gelatin in his presence. All that tattooed skin—muscles bulging in that sensual, uniquely Pacific island way—the pale brownness offset by slightly elongated, sapphire-blue eyes, features like an exotic cat in the firelight. Gorgeous. Untouchable.

Or was he…

Again the finger beckoned, that of the bare-chested dream man, his hair blacker than the sky, pouring untamed down his corded back.

Her imagination ran wild with possibilities. None of them G-rated, none of them even remotely realistic.

"Go on, Sefy," urged her troublemaking girlfriend Stacy, pushing her forward into the fire-ringed circle. "He wants you."

"Yea, come on," agreed the equally traitorous Debbie. "Live a little. It's our last night on the island."

They held her upper arms, preventing her planned escape back to the relative safety of her hotel room. "I am living," she squealed, digging her bare heels into the sand. "Quite happily, I might add."

"As an old maid, maybe," snorted Stacy, who'd roped her not only into viewing this corny outdoor dance show, but the entire week's island vacation as well—a vacation, which, in Persephone's opinion, had been a colossal waste of time and money. "Now are you going out there or do we have to confiscate your PDA and your laptop till we get home?"

"You wouldn't dare and besides..."

Sefy's arguments, and everything else on her mind fizzled as he took her hand. It was not merely a holding of her flesh, but an enveloping, the fingers warm and firm, so much bigger and stronger, entirely possessing hers and yet not in the least bit threatening.

I will never hurt you, the fingers said, but watch out because I'm interested in you and I may not want to let you go.

Sefy's feet were powerless as he eased her forward, into his orbit. He stopped her just short of himself, settling her into a position and proximity that made the rest of the world spin away into insignificance, a galaxy or more away.

His body was like a carnival to her eyes. Everywhere she looked were delights to capture her attention, from the tiny gold rings inserted in his masculine nipples to the incredible array of body designs, gorgeous patterns covering one whole arm, his torso and most of his hard, powerful thighs and legs.

The ink was black and blue and red and green and she could just lose herself looking at the fire flickering over the ever-changing figures, creatures and symbols. What did they all mean? She wanted to know them all. More than that, Sefy wanted to kiss and lick every inch of his delectable skin. Was that the influence of the silly umbrella drinks, she wondered, or just the result of a starved libido?

How long had it been since anyone had made love to her?

He was saying something to her now, smiling coyly.

She couldn't understand a word, but who cared? Just watching those full, masculine lips move, each and every syllable radiating outward like invisible fire, the cheekbones high, but not feminine, the jaw strong, masculine and bold, was a heaven all its own.

An enigma. That's what this man was.

And he was beautiful, too. Had she mentioned that?

"Fire dancer say he want to make dance with you," interpreted the curly haired, Hawaiian shirted character with the swelled, poi poi belly who'd been acting as master of ceremonies for the torchlight tourist show. "Special treat, just for you. Called *Lu-atey*."

That must be Polynesian for 'embarrass the socks off the tourist girl', she thought.

"Lady like to dance?"

"Hell, yes!" Stacy answered for her.

"Go on," coached Debbie. "Tell him."

Sefy nodded just to shut them up, winning an immediate wink from the beautiful tattooed man that made her blush from head to toe. Standing here before such a strong, virile creature, she felt entirely too underdressed and underprotected in her lemon yellow bikini and sheer wrap.

"Hey, everybody," the announcer chanted in his charmingly broken English. "How 'bout big hand for pretty lady. She big sport, right?"

Sefy could hear Debbie and Stacy squealing in the background, leading the crowd of about fifty in a healthy round of applause. Really, she'd never done anything like this in her life. A bookworm all through school, and now a grown-up international banker, she'd shunned the limelight and the party life. Everyone else told her she was wasting her natural good looks, but as far as she was concerned, her long, wheat-colored hair and mannequin shaped figure only got in the way of serious pursuits.

"Dance begin with girl," said the announcer. "Girl move hips, show to man."

Persephone felt the heat rise to her cheeks. She hadn't bargained on being put on exhibit right off the bat.

"Come on, Sefy!"

"You go, girl."

Great; her own personal rooting section of sadists.

Persephone made a pathetic, minimalist effort. With any luck she'd be booed right off the stage, ending the thing before it began.

The tattooed hunk had other ideas, however. Catching her entirely off guard, he reached for her slender waist; his large hands lightning fast in the superheated air. Sefy gasped as he did the hip moving for her, demonstrating exactly what it was women did that looked so good to him and the rest of his gender. She ought to be infuriated that he was touching her without permission, but it kind of turned her on that he hadn't asked, that he'd been bold enough to seize her body and do with it what he liked.

Besides, who could argue with a man who looked like him?

As long as things didn't get out of hand. Again, she was aware of too much nudity, the hard heat of him burning her flesh through the intervening air as their crotches gyrated in synchronous movement. It was clear he was being careful, holding her at arm's length so as not to touch his sex to hers, but there was no denying her all too easily available flesh. It was a decidedly one-sided situation. She herself would never dare reach for his loincloth, and yet she knew the fire dancer could strip her in a matter of seconds, rendering her nude to his gaze or anything else he might wish to impose.

"Girl move good," commented the microphone man.

Sefy was beyond hearing the cheers of the audience. He had drawn her in, and there was no way back. It was in his eyes: the beating of her own life force, and in the touch of his strong hands, the strength of which was giving her the power to stay on her feet. For some reason, this man had suddenly become the center of her world.

Desperately, now, she looked to the lines of his smile for the approval she needed and craved. Was she really doing this right? Was he sorry he'd picked her and not one of the other girls—either of her sexy girlfriends or maybe one of the lovely native girls, all of whom were so much prettier than her?

"Second part of dance. Man see backside."

A flood of insecurity washed over Sefy, mingled with more than a tinge of resentment. Why was she the sex object here? Why was it always this way for the female? Maybe she'd like to inspect his ass for a while.

Before she could register a protest, the fire dancer lifted her off her feet and whirled her like a ballerina. Sefy felt a play toy to him and that just made her madder. He was a bully, that's what he was.

"*Lu-atay* is very old dance," the narrator was saying. "Once upon a time, it was used for sacred purpose by island prince. For selecting mate; woman known as an *isina*, who would submit to him in all things and live with him forever."

Sefy's ears perked up, her brain re-activating back out of what was dangerously resembling blonde bimbo mode.

Had he just mentioned submission?

Enjoy this excerpt from
Come and Get Me
© Copyright Reese Gabriel, 2005

All Rights Reserved, Ellora's Cave Publishing, Inc.

Eleesha was already five minutes late when she saw the motorcycle. Sleek, red and futuristic...and parked in *her* spot! She cursed both her bad luck and the owner's insensitive, uncaring behavior. How hard could if be to read a reserved parking sign written in plain English? She'd bet anything the culprit was a man.

Forced to round the corner to the side of the building, Eleesha settled on a place three rows back in the crowded lot. Slapping on an extra layer of nuke-proof lip gloss for insurance and double checking her precariously ordered auburn curls, she hopped out of her sedan and hightailed it for the weekly department head meeting of Global Tech, Inc, already in progress.

Her navy blue heels were not cooperating. Neither they nor the slinky suit skirt she'd chosen this particular Monday were intended for a hundred yard dash across pitted blacktop. Of all days to have to face the visiting corporate efficiency consultant, she thought. Of course this all might have been avoided if Chester, her lovingly annoying Siamese cat, hadn't chosen to walk all over her alarm in the middle of the night, rendering it silent at wakeup time.

Chester was a male, too.

"Good morning, Miss Greene," nodded Frank, the security man at the front desk.

"Morning, Frank," she blurred past the kindly, white-haired guard.

Invariably, her mind went into free association. Frank. Security. The motorcycle. *Justice*.

Eleesha skidded to a halt halfway down the corridor. "Frank, someone's in my spot," she called out. "Send for a tow truck, would you please?"

Frank's snow-white eyebrows knitted nervously. "Well, um, actually Miss Greene, I can't do that."

She was back at the reception desk in a flash. Meeting or no meeting, she was going to sort this out. "What do you mean you can't? Someone's hijacked my place and I demand satisfaction."

"Actually..." corrected a confidant bordering on arrogant, smooth male voice behind her, "you can't technically hijack a parking place."

The ill-timed intrusion managed to snap Eleesha's last remaining nerve. "Excuse me," she whirled around to confront him, "but I don't believe I'm in need of any grammar les—"

Eleesha's exclamation fizzled mid-word. Her mouth hung open in blatant disbelief. This was no ordinary interruption she was dealing with. This was an unmitigated disaster. An unwanted, bad trip down memory lane.

"Hello, Eleesha," said Ross Maclean, the man who'd taken full and complete possession of her body for one scorching, unforgettable night a decade ago in college. "Long time no see."

She fought the flush in her face. The last time he'd seen her she'd been nude, panting on his bed, begging to be allowed to come as he tortured her maddeningly with his huge, pulsing erection, sliding it agonizingly slowly in and out of her slick, gaping sex. He'd won her that night in a game, a bizarre sorority ritual called Come and Get Me, which made the pledges into sexual door prizes for the big time jocks.

"Ross," she acknowledged, trying to keep her tone neutral. Already, she could feel her body responding to him, the dampness between her legs, the quickening of her pulse. How could it be that her pussy still remembered the exact shape of him, the exact length and thickness? How could it be that she remembered his taste, salty sweet as he let her lick his hardness, 'til it pulsed with need too great to ignore? The taste of her, too, on his lips as he kissed her after tonguing her swollen sex. One word, she feared, one motion of his fingers and she might be tearing at her clothes, ready to give in to him all over again.

If only he'd gotten ugly, old or fat. As it was, the intervening time had done absolutely nothing to diminish the raw masculine beauty of the former quarterback. His hair was thick and brown, brushed neatly back and trimmed around his ears. His face was ruggedly handsome, featuring cerulean blue eyes, a dimpled chin and a firm, decisive jawline. He was wearing well-worn blue jeans, which he filled out to perfection, along with a green t-shirt under a brown flight jacket.

She nearly swooned at the scent of him. So familiar...musk, mixed with pure testosterone. It was like being back in college, all those times she'd followed him around her freshman year. She'd been barely eighteen. He'd been a twenty-two-year-old senior—tall, dark and heroic—bound for the NFL. She'd have done anything to get his attention, and one day she'd finally gotten her chance.

Though not quite as she'd imagined.

About the author:

Reese Gabriel is a born romantic with a taste for the edgier side of love. Having traveled the world and sampled many of the finer things, Reese now enjoys the greater simplicities; barefoot walks by the ocean, kisses under moonlight and whispers of passion in the darkness with that one special person.

Preferring to remain behind the scenes, cherished by a precious few, Reese hopes to awaken in the lives of many the possibilities of true love through stories of far off places and enchanted lives.

For the sake of love and hope and imagination, these stories are told. May they be enjoyed as much in the reading of them as in the writing.

Reese Gabriel welcomes mail from readers. You can write to Reese c/o Ellora's Cave Publishing at 1056 Home Avenue, Akron OH 44310-3502.

Why an electronic book?

We live in the Information Age—an exciting time in the history of human civilization in which technology rules supreme and continues to progress in leaps and bounds every minute of every hour of every day. For a multitude of reasons, more and more avid literary fans are opting to purchase e-books instead of paperbacks. The question to those not yet initiated to the world of electronic reading is simply: *why?*

1. *Price.* An electronic title at Ellora's Cave Publishing and Cerridwen Press runs anywhere from 40-75% less than the cover price of the <u>exact same title</u> in paperback format. Why? Cold mathematics. It is less expensive to publish an e-book than it is to publish a paperback, so the savings are passed along to the consumer.

2. *Space.* Running out of room to house your paperback books? That is one worry you will never have with electronic novels. For a low one-time cost, you can purchase a handheld computer designed specifically for e-reading purposes. Many e-readers are larger than the average handheld, giving you plenty of screen room. Better yet, hundreds of titles can be stored within your new library—a single microchip. (Please note that Ellora's Cave and Cerridwen Press does not endorse any specific brands. You can check our website at www.ellorascave.com or

www.cerridwenpress.com for customer recommendations we make available to new consumers.)

3. *Mobility.* Because your new library now consists of only a microchip, your entire cache of books can be taken with you wherever you go.

4. *Personal preferences are accounted for.* Are the words you are currently reading too small? Too large? Too...**ANNOYING**? Paperback books cannot be modified according to personal preferences, but e-books can.

5. *Instant gratification.* Is it the middle of the night and all the bookstores are closed? Are you tired of waiting days—sometimes weeks—for online and offline bookstores to ship the novels you bought? Ellora's Cave Publishing sells instantaneous downloads 24 hours a day, 7 days a week, 365 days a year. Our e-book delivery system is 100% automated, meaning your order is filled as soon as you pay for it.

Those are a few of the top reasons why electronic novels are displacing paperbacks for many an avid reader. As always, Ellora's Cave and Cerridwen Press welcomes your questions and comments. We invite you to email us at service@ellorascave.com, service@cerridwenpress.com or write to us directly at: 1056 Home Ave. Akron OH 44310-3502.

ELLORA'S CAVE
ROMANTICA PUBLISHING

Discover for yourself why readers can't get enough of the multiple award-winning publisher Ellora's Cave. Whether you prefer e-books or paperbacks, be sure to visit EC on the web at www.ellorascave.com for an erotic reading experience that will leave you breathless.

www.ellorascave.com